KW-217-596

Large Print

Linford Romance Library

Mary Jane Warmington

MISTRESS of ELVAN HALL

STANHOPE
627591

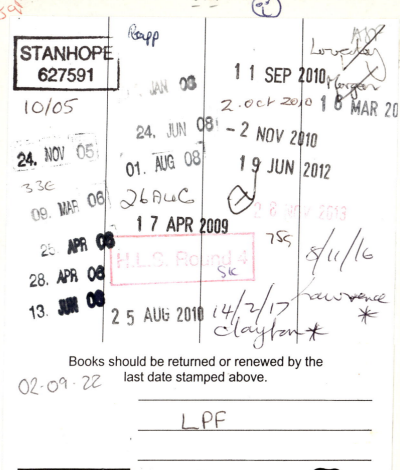

Books should be returned or renewed by the
last date stamped above.

LPF

CUSTOMER SERVICE EXCELLENCE

00884\DTP\RN\04.05

C152555101

SPECIAL MESSAGE TO READERS

This book is published under the auspices of

THE ULVERSCROFT FOUNDATION

(registered charity No. 264873 UK)

Established in 1972 to provide funds for research, diagnosis and treatment of eye diseases. Examples of contributions made are: —

A Children's Assessment Unit at Moorfield's Hospital, London.

•

Twin operating theatres at the Western Ophthalmic Hospital, London.

•

A Chair of Ophthalmology at the Royal Australian College of Ophthalmologists.

•

The Ulverscroft Children's Eye Unit at the Great Ormond Street Hospital For Sick Children, London.

You can help further the work of the Foundation by making a donation or leaving a legacy. Every contribution, no matter how small, is received with gratitude. Please write for details to:

**THE ULVERSCROFT FOUNDATION,
The Green, Bradgate Road, Anstey,
Leicester LE7 7FU, England.
Telephone: (0116) 236 4325**

In Australia write to:
**THE ULVERSCROFT FOUNDATION,
c/o The Royal Australian College of
Ophthalmologists,
27, Commonwealth Street, Sydney,
N.S.W. 2010.**

MISTRESS OF ELVAN HALL

Anne loved Francis so much that she was prepared to marry him on any terms, but she was only too well aware that Francis loved only Elvan Hall. Or did he? Where did Caroline Cook fit in? She was beautiful, she was obviously head over heels in love with Francis — yet he had not married her. Why not? What had made him choose Anne for his wife, and not this other girl who would have been so much more suitable?

Books by Mary Jane Warmington
in the Linford Romance Library:

NURSE VICTORIA
WILD POPPY
THE STRANGERS AT BRIERY HALL

MARY JANE WARMINGTON

MISTRESS OF ELVAN HALL

Complete and Unabridged

LINFORD
Leicester

First published in Great Britain
under the name of
'Mary Cummins'

First Linford Edition
published 2000

All the characters in this book have no existence
outside the imagination of the Author,
and have no relation whatsoever to anyone
bearing the same name or names. They are
not even distantly inspired by any individual
known or unknown to the Author, and all
the incidents are pure invention.

Copyright © 1972 by Mary Cummins
All rights reserved

British Library CIP Data

Warmington, Mary Jane
    Mistress of Elvan Hall.—Large print ed.—
    Linford romance library
    1. Love stories
    2. Large type books
    I. Title II. Cummins, Mary
    823.9′14 [F]

    ISBN 0–7089–5663–7

KENT
ARTS & LIBRARIES

C\52555101

Published by
F. A. Thorpe (Publishing)
Anstey, Leicestershire

Set by Words & Graphics Ltd.
Anstey, Leicestershire
Printed and bound in Great Britain by
T. J. International Ltd., Padstow, Cornwall

This book is printed on acid-free paper

1

Anne Drummond climbed a small hill, then lay flat out on the grass, gazing down on the quiet valley which had been her birthplace. Soon her father would retire from the old Manse where he had been minister to the parish of Arndale for almost quarter of a century, and go with Nell, his wife, to the small cottage they had bought on the Ayrshire coast in preparation for his retirement.

Anne sighed, thinking that an era of her life was now coming to a close. The fact that the cottage was too small to hold three had not troubled her, because she had been engaged to Graham Lord, whom she had known all her life. Graham's father, Dr. Lord, had also served Arndale for as many years as Stephen Drummond. The two children had been brought up together

1

and their parents had often smiled indulgently at their close relationship. Anne and Graham were ideally matched, in their opinion.

They had become engaged after Graham, too, had qualified as a doctor, and Anne had just started her first job as secretary to Francis Wyatt of the Wyatt Engineering Company in Carlisle. Three weeks ago she had handed over her job to another girl, her wedding to Graham being eagerly awaited by the whole of Arndale, then two days before the wedding, Graham had backed out.

'It's no good, is it, Anne?' he asked her, having taken her in his arms to kiss her goodnight, then released her abruptly.

'What's no good?' she asked.

'You and me. You especially. You don't really love me, Anne. Oh, I know you love me in a way, but not real love . . . not as I want it to be.'

She stared at him in the fading light. 'I don't know what you mean,

Graham,' she whispered.

'Oh yes, you do. I can feel you stiffen against me whenever I try to kiss you properly. You're only marrying me because it's what has been expected of us for years. At first you were happy to go along with it, but not any more. I can feel the change in you, Anne.'

Her knees began to tremble a little.

'Change?'

Graham reached out and held her close again.

'It's all right, darling. Don't think I'm angry. Only nobody is going to force you into marriage if it isn't right for you, even if it's marriage to me. You hate to disappoint your father and mother, especially your father, who wants to see you settled.'

They were both quiet for a moment. They both knew that Stephen Drummond's health wasn't at its best these days. Dr. Lord's eyes had often been anxious as they rested on his old friend.

'And my folks are every bit as bad,' Graham said wryly.

3

'How . . . how long have you felt like this?' Anne asked. 'Couldn't you have spoken before . . . before the arrangements went so far?'

A small smile twisted Graham's mouth.

'I wasn't sure before. Now I am. And besides, I thought you'd be the one to call it off. There's someone else important to you, isn't there, Anne? Could it be Francis Wyatt?'

She threw her head back as though he had stung her cheek.

'No!' she cried. 'What a thing to ask! Mr. Wyatt is . . . was . . . my employer. How could you think such a thing!'

'Because I saw you with him in Carlisle just before you left Wyatt's for good. You and he were having a cup of coffee in a restaurant there, and I saw you . . . you were at a table just by the window. I almost rushed in to speak to you, then I saw your face, Anne. It was a shock, I've had to wait a little to decide whether or not it was true. You've fallen in love with

4

him, haven't you, my dear?'

Anne swallowed.

'I don't know,' she said huskily. 'It's hopeless anyway. He doesn't even notice me. I'm only the girl at the typewriter. That day ... that day we were working on a special order and he was rather worried. I think he had home worries, too. I ... I was sorry for him, Graham. I hated to see him upset. He hides his worries so well, but I always know ...'

'You're in love with him, that's why you know,' repeated Graham. 'I can't take the chance on marrying you while your heart belongs to someone else.'

Anne drew a long breath, and looked squarely at Graham. She had been trying to hide from the truth ever since she had left Wyatt's. There had been a great gaping hole in her life as she walked out of the quiet offices, resigning her desk and chair to Louise Dalton, Francis Wyatt's new secretary.

Now she knew that Graham was holding up the truth to her like a bright mirror, so that she could see it reflected clearly for the first time.

'And you, Graham?' she asked. 'What about you? Have we both been pushed into marriage, do you think?'

He grinned.

'It's all been mapped out for us since our cradles. I don't think we're ready for it, Anne. I'm no more ready for marriage than you are to marry me. No doubt I'll fall properly in love some day with someone else, too. Are you willing to be brave, Anne darling? Shall we be ourselves for once and tell them to stop ringing those wedding bells? Can you go through all the fag of returning those presents? I'll help, you know, and so will your mother when she sees we mean it. Our parents aren't ogres, but they are wishful thinkers, my dear. Shall we give ourselves an uncomfortable week and avoid making the mistake of our lives?'

Anne's eyes searched his for the truth, and saw that Graham meant every word. He wasn't just thinking of her. He was thinking of himself, too. He wasn't yet ready for marriage.

'All right,' she agreed. 'It's a deal. And Graham — I *do* love you.'

He paused for a moment, then his eyes twinkled.

'And I love you,' he assured her. 'Never more so than now. We'll always be friends, won't we?'

'Always,' she agreed happily.

'Look, darling, if you want that chap, why don't you grab him?'

Anne's eyes widened.

'Oh, Graham, you don't know what you're talking about.'

'Don't I? Listen, my sweet, you can grab any chap you want, take it from Uncle Graham. In fact, even now I'm tempted to tell you it was all a mistake, and let's keep to the original arrangement. Oh, don't panic! I can see all this has come as a relief to you, but seriously . . . he's not married, is he?'

'No, but . . .'

'Then the best of luck. I'll keep in

touch. And remember, if you want him, grab him.'

Anne watched Graham go, a smile playing about her lips, then she remembered the task ahead. How to undo the strings of a life which had become rather tangled.

It had been hard convincing their parents and Stephen Drummond had taken the news harder than anyone. Anne could see the anxiety in her mother's eyes as they followed her husband who was looking thin and frail.

'Don't worry, Mummy,' Anne comforted her. 'Daddy's just tired. He'll be much better at the cottage and he can write heaps more of his books for small boys. You know how he loves that.'

'I know, dear,' said Mrs. Drummond. 'They've been profitable, too. They've practically bought the cottage. But . . . but, Anne, what will you do? You know . . . '

'I know and it's all right, really. You won't want a daughter of my age parked on you at the cottage for always.

It's far too tiny to hold three of us permanently. No, I'll get another job.'

'Back at Wyatt's?'

'No,' said Anne quickly, then continued more gently, seeing the surprise in her mother's eyes, 'No, Mummy. My place has been filled, don't forget. I returned my wedding gift to Mr. Wyatt, of course, but I can't ask for my job back. Anyway, I may try somewhere else instead of Carlisle . . . Ayr, perhaps. Then I wouldn't be far away from you and Daddy.'

'That would be lovely, darling,' said Mrs. Drummond, rather absently. Anne knew that already she was again thinking about Stephen and planning how to save him from stress and strain over the few short weeks till his retirement. The parish had been disappointed over her wedding, and Stephen Drummond felt that the disappointment reflected on him.

'I'll contact an agency tomorrow,' Anne promised. 'I'll get fixed up again as soon as I can.'

Anne had written many letters, but the replies had been disappointing, and she had come out to her favourite spot, a grassy slope on the hill overlooking Arndale, in order to think things out.

She could not go back to Wyatt's. If Graham had guessed at the strong emotion which had grown in her for Francis Wyatt, could it be that Francis himself had also guessed and had welcomed her resignation with relief? Anne's cheeks burned at the thought.

Yet he had accepted the fact that she was leaving in order to marry Graham with detachment, asking few questions, and wishing her a future of great happiness, as though he cared what happened to her.

He had always been a considerate employer, even in times of stress, and Anne remembered the only occasion when she had glimpsed another Francis Wyatt behind the careful, competent business man.

'Have you always lived in Dumfriesshire, Miss Drummond?' he asked, and she nodded.

'Always.'

'Your father is a minister of the church?'

'At Arndale. He's . . . not very well at the moment and is seeking an early retirement. He has a secondary occupation.'

This time small dimples showed in her cheeks, and she brushed back her soft honey-coloured hair, smiling at him with warm brown eyes.

'He writes books for small boys of eight to eleven. They're rather popular and they give Daddy a lot of pleasure as well. They're full of exciting adventures among the planets, and no doubt teach young boys the relative size and distance of each planet, one from another.'

His dark eyes were full of interest as he listened, and he looked suddenly much younger as he grinned, while she described the latest book.

11

'I type his manuscripts each weekend when I go home,' she explained. 'The illustrations occupy a large part of the book.'

'Your father does these as well?'

'He trained in art before he became ordained.'

'I see. Then you aren't artistic?'

She blushed.

'A little, perhaps, but my talent isn't good enough to earn me my living at art, so I settled for something much more mundane. I settled for a secretarial training.'

'I see.'

He was thoughtful for a moment.

'Do you have an eye for beauty, though . . . I mean beauty of landscape, of snow-capped mountains against a blue sky, of ancient trees which adorn themselves with new leaves year after year, of old and beautiful buildings which have grown into that landscape?'

She felt he was speaking more to himself than to her.

'Do you know Cumberland at all, Miss Drummond?'

She shook her head.

'Not very well. I've had little opportunity of getting to know other places so far.'

He was silent for a long time while she studied his lean dark face with well-cut black hair, straight eyebrows and a nose which could give his features a hawklike appearance when he was troubled. Looking back, she knew now that she had been aware, then, of his attraction for her. She had tried to tell herself that her feelings for him were loyalty and affection for someone she held in great respect, and that her real love was for Graham. But she knew now that Graham was right, and she had already lost her heart to Francis Wyatt.

'My home is there,' he told her, 'near Cockermouth. It's an old house, very old, in fact. The Wyatts have lived there for generations. Time was when the Elvan estate spread over many acres, but those days have gone, though many people would consider Elvan Hall a sizeable property for the present day.

'My mother lives there now, with my two younger sisters. Helen is nineteen and Judith only eleven. My grandfather founded Wyatt Engineering, since the estate isn't self-supporting. In fact . . . ' he paused for a moment, 'the house requires a great deal of attention. My mother . . . well, she has her own ideas as to what requires to be done. I . . . I have to approve of her plans before they can be carried out.'

His eyebrows suddenly looked dark as his brows wrinkled.

'I love Elvan Hall, Miss Drummond. I'm concerned to . . . to be a good steward and see that my descendants have a home of beauty which can be handed on. My forebears have done as much for me.'

'Of course,' agreed Anne. 'I suppose anyone who didn't appreciate such a heritage could do irreparable harm.'

'Yes,' he agreed, and there was a rather harsh note in his voice. 'Irreparable harm.'

* * *

Elvan Hall had caught at Anne's imagination and she often fancied she could see the old grey-stone house, against a background of lawns, old stout trees and smoky blue hills, with the clear sparkling river winding past. In spring wild flowers grew in abundance along the river banks, and the woods were full of snowdrops followed by daffodils.

Then Anne would remember Mrs. Wyatt, a rather fluffy-looking woman in her fifties, who could nevertheless be autocratic. She had turned up unexpectedly at the office one day, and had made Anne feel small and insignificant, even in her role as private secretary to Francis Wyatt. She had seen the quiet controlled patience on his face as he listened to his mother's demands, and had guessed that although he loved and respected her, she put her own comfort and feelings before his.

'She loves herself more than him,' thought Anne, and wondered if it was because she obviously had not got him under her thumb. He was his own master.

But there was something lacking in his life, even though she had never again been allowed to glimpse behind the façade. There was something wrong about his home life. Even though her own home was sometimes beset by anxieties, it was nevertheless a place of love. It was that love which had helped her to face up to the curiosity of outsiders when she and Graham called off their marriage.

Anne sighed and pulled a blade of grass. She would not be an encumbrance to her parents, of that she was determined. She had a small amount of savings, and might even go to London where she was sure she could get a job.

16

Besides, she loved London and could be happy there.

She paused as she chewed her blade of grass and stared down at a flash of colour in the Manse garden. Her mother had hung out something brilliantly red on the clothes-line, and with a lithe movement Anne was on her feet. The red article, which she suspected was her old swim-suit, was a signal since her schooldays that she was wanted urgently at home.

Anne brushed down her tweed skirt and zipped up her anorak, then set off at a pace. No doubt some well-meaning lady of the parish had come to call, and to reassure herself and her friends that Anne's heart wasn't broken, and that her marriage really had been called off by mutual consent.

Anne never resented interference of this kind, knowing that it was born of regard for her and her family.

Nevertheless, she thought with a sigh, it wasn't easy to face the probing with a natural smile, without showing *any* resentment. She quickened her steps. The sooner she got it over the better.

She took the path through the back garden and into the house through the kitchen door, passing her red swim-suit which flopped garishly on the clothes-line. Her mother was brewing coffee and setting out cups on her best tray.

'Who is it?' asked Anne, peeling off her anorak. 'Miss Simpson or Mrs. Clegg?'

'Neither,' said Mrs. Drummond, a speculative look in her eye. 'It's Mr. Wyatt . . . for you.'

Anne gulped and turned to stare at her mother, the blood rushing to her cheeks while her hands sought her hair and tried to brush down her skirt at the same time.

'Oh, goodness! And just look at me — all covered with grass!'

The speculative look her mother was giving her deepened. Was this the real reason behind the sudden calling-off of a wedding which had been arranged for

18

years? Surely Anne would not be foolish enough to lose Graham because of someone like Francis Wyatt . . . someone beyond her reach?

'Have you written to ask for your job back?' she asked, as casually as she could. 'I know you hadn't intended to.'

'I told you it had been filled,' said Anne, trying to keep patient. 'You know I couldn't ask to go back, Mother.'

'Well, he seems determined to see you, because he said he would wait until you came home, however long you were away. Your father is entertaining him in the drawing room, showing him some of his published books.' Mrs. Drummond's face suddenly softened into a smile. 'He's rather a charming man, really. He was genuinely delighted to look at those books, as though he had missed reading that sort of thing as a boy. I always find it rather touching to see a boy peeping out of a strong, dignified type of man. Look, dear, if you want to clean up, I'll hold the fort, only don't be long.'

'Thanks, Mummy. I only want to wash my face and change my skirt and shoes.'

Anne looked fresh and lovely when she appeared a few minutes later in the drawing room, and Francis Wyatt leapt to his feet as he shook her hand.

'I . . . er . . . I was sorry to have news of your . . . er . . . your broken engagement,' he told her, the colour suddenly high in his cheeks.

Anne nodded briefly, and made little comment. Mr. Wyatt wasn't very good at discussing personal affairs. He was much more sure of himself rapping out business letters which were always very lucid.

'It was by mutual consent,' she said. 'Graham and I are very fond of one another, but not enough to marry. We're like . . . ' she glanced at her parents, ' . . . brother and sister, to coin a phrase.'

Stephen Drummond frowned.

'But you aren't related, and it was always understood . . . '

'I know, but that was before we were old enough to fall in love . . . '

She broke off, her cheeks colouring, aware of Francis Wyatt's eyes on her.

'Graham is too young to be tied down yet, anyway. He wants to enjoy his freedom a while,' she said, tossing her pale honey-coloured hair. 'We understand each other perfectly.'

'It's better to back out, then, before it's too late,' put in Nell Drummond, trying to be helpful, and her husband sighed deeply.

'I suppose so. Young people please themselves these days, anyway. I think we had a more stable society when everyone obeyed the rules. Don't you agree, Mr. Wyatt?'

'Oh, certainly, certainly,' said Francis, though Anne was glancing at him rather curiously. Had her successor, Louise Dalton, proved to be unsuitable after all? He was not the easiest of employers, but Louise had seemed the very soul of efficiency, one of those girls who really loved secretarial work.

Anne had often thought that she had chosen that for herself because it seemed the more suitable from an earning point of view. She had been good at it because it was in her nature to do things well, but she had not really loved the job. This crossroads in her life had made her wonder if she couldn't take a different path.

Yet here was Francis Wyatt seeking her out again, and it was more than possible that he would ask her to come back.

What should she say? she asked herself, trying to merge into the background and view him dispassionately as he discussed present-day trends with her parents. She loved him. She loved his lean dark face and long slender fingers with bony wrists appearing from under his immaculate cuffs. She loved the straight look he often gave her from his dark eyes which could sometimes gleam with humour, but were more often full of thought. His father had died when he was barely out of his teens and his youngest sister a small child. He'd had precious little time to be a boy. He'd had to grow up too soon, thought Anne sadly. He hadn't had enough fun in his life.

'You can talk in here, then,' her mother was saying. 'Is that all right, Anne?'

She came out of her dreams with a start, aware that all three were looking at her questioningly.

'Ah . . . yes, yes,' she replied, unwilling to admit that she had missed half of what had been said.

'Come on then, Stephen my dear. Help me carry the tray.'

The older man got up a trifle reluctantly, his stooped figure showing frailty.

'I'll carry the tray,' offered Francis. 'Here, let me do it, Mrs. Drummond.'

He took the tray from her and followed her to the kitchen. Stephen turned and looked at his daughter.

'It isn't easy to decide about new

23

paths, my dear,' he said gently. 'Sometimes the old well-trodden ones are best. Sometimes new ones are pitted with holes.'

And sometimes they lead to treasures unknown, thought Anne, though she didn't say so. A rush of affection for her father made tears prick her eyelids. He had been disappointed when she and Graham called off their marriage, but only because of his concern for her.

'I know, Daddy,' she whispered, kissing him. 'But working for Mr. Wyatt *is* an old path, don't forget.'

'Ah . . . work,' murmured Mr. Drummond. 'Girls were meant to be home-makers, not workers. Here's Mr. Wyatt now.'

He held the door open for Francis, then closed it behind both of them, and Anne was face to face with the man she loved for the first time since she left the office.

'Shall . . . shall we sit down again by the fire?' she offered nervously, and he nodded his agreement. Again the heightened colour was in his cheeks, and she felt that he was as nervous as she. This, oddly enough, served to calm her down, and she smiled pleasantly as she drew up a chair for him.

'Now,' she commanded, 'tell me why you've come.'

Francis Wyatt hitched forward a little on his chair, then regarded Anne gravely.

'Your marriage . . . did not take place, then . . . ' he said slowly.

'No. But there's no need for you to feel responsible for me in any way. I know my position has been filled. I take it that Miss Dalton is proving efficient?'

Francis nodded, though his thoughts seemed elsewhere.

'Very efficient. She oils the wheels very effectively. Er . . . please don't think me impertinent, but was the decision to call off your marriage really by mutual consent?'

'Of course,' she said quickly. 'Graham is really too young for marriage. He's a man, certainly, but he

25

wants to get to know the world a little before he's tied to a small corner of it. We're the same age, you know, but women are usually more ready to settle down than men . . . though perhaps not so much nowadays.'

'And you let him go.'

'Of course,' she said crisply.

She was becoming nervous of his searching questions, afraid of betraying the true reason behind her break with Graham. She clasped her hands and threw back the heavy golden hair, with a small toss of her head, then smiled at him.

'As I say, you mustn't feel responsible for me, Mr. Wyatt.'

He frowned.

'How long have you worked for me, Miss Drummond?'

'Two . . . almost two years.'

'Two years. We . . . got to know one another quite well. I found you a soothing influence on my life. I felt your . . . understanding. I need someone like you. In fact, I need you at Elvan Hall.'

So it was another job! Anne bit her lips as she began to assimilate what that would mean. Francis Wyatt often stayed at his flat in Carlisle during the week and was only home at weekends, and during the week she would be at the beck and call of his mother.

Anne remembered Mrs. Wyatt and recoiled a little. How could she work for a woman like her, who probably treated her underlings high-handedly, and whose orders were likely to be ill-considered in the first place?

'I . . . er . . . at Elvan Hall?' she queried hesitantly.

'The house requires to be renovated, as I explained to you once before. It hasn't been touched for some years, but care must be taken in order that the age and character of the house be preserved. I . . . I feel that you would love my home, and appreciate its beauty. I know that I would be happier to leave on my trip to America if I thought you were at Elvan Hall.'

'You're going to America?'

He nodded. 'The contract we were negotiating is ours, but there are many problems to be ironed out. I shall be away for several weeks.'

Her heart unaccountably sank. Only now did she realise what balm it had been just to see him again, and now he was going away. Anne drew a deep breath. He could have no idea how she felt, or he wouldn't ask her to stay at his home.

'I doubt if I could be of much use to you helping with renovations. I'm not an interior designer or anything like that . . .'

'That has all been done. It's a matter of carrying out the work.'

'Surely your mother . . .'

'My mother did not entirely approve of proposals which had my full support. She has ideas of her own. I . . . I don't want any changes made while I'm away. Please understand, there is much in the house to treasure and to preserve. A mistress of the house can leave her own mark, but she must be aware of what can be tastefully changed and what can be desecrated. It's no ordinary house. That's why I can't even offer you a free hand, though I know, from knowing you, that you'd understand.'

Again Anne bit her lip. She would have no authority in the house to stop Mrs. Wyatt desecrating whatever she liked. She tried to put this point of view to Francis.

'But I'd have no authority over your mother.'

Francis Wyatt's eyes looked very black as he gazed at her.

'You would . . . as my wife,' he said quietly.

Anne wondered if she had heard aright.

'As your wife?' she asked stupidly.

He leaned forward eagerly.

'Yes. I've thought about it so much, Anne, and wondered if it would be fair to you. But it's a heritage, you see. I feel you have it in you to love it all as I do.'

'But one ought to love a person for marriage, not a house,' she said, almost in a whisper. 'One doesn't marry for love of a house.'

The colour crept slowly up in his checks, then receded again, leaving his face very white.

'You couldn't marry without love, Anne? Is that what you're telling me?'

She was about to shake her head, then she paused, very much aware of standing at those crossroads her father had mentioned. She could send him away and keep to her well-trodden path, or she could go down a new unknown way, which could be full of pitfalls, but which might also have glories unknown with Francis by her side. Her love for him was almost overwhelming her, but would it be strong enough to live through future years if he had only liking, and respect . . . affection even . . . in return?

Yet other marriages had succeeded, which had been based on reasons other than love. She had yet to see Elvan Hall, but she remembered drinking in every detail eagerly, when Francis talked about it. He had been aware of her interest, and her love for beauty which had been cherished through the ages.

'Is it so important?' he was aking again.

'Are you offering me an ordinary marriage? I mean, would you prefer a marriage in name only?'

The colour flooded her checks and she saw the tension in him.

'No,' he said at length. 'It could only be an . . . ordinary marriage. I would want you for my wife in every way. I only wanted to know if you were still in love with Graham Lord. I'm asking you to marry me, but I'd be happier if your heart was . . . well, free.'

She didn't know what to say. He was offering her a true marriage, but there was no word of love for her.

'And you?' she asked. 'Is your heart free?'

Again his eyes grew dark, and he was very still.

'I couldn't marry anyone else but

you, Anne,' he told her, rather harshly, and she felt he had not answered her question. It could easily mean that he loved someone else who was out of his reach.

'I can't give you time to think about it. There's no time. If you agree, then we must be married as soon as ever possible. Your . . . your father can perhaps arrange it. I suppose I should first have approached your parents, but I had to talk to you first. Besides . . . ' he rubbed his forehead, 'besides, I'm very bad at this sort of thing.'

He smiled ruefully and she could see the strain which had been put upon him. Her heart almost turned over as his eyes softened, looking into hers and she felt there was nothing she wouldn't do to help him, and protect him. Half a loaf was always better than no bread, she thought, and tried to convince herself that this was no ordinary man asking a girl to be his wife. She was also being asked to be the mistress of Elvan Hall.

'I'll marry you whenever it can be arranged,' she told him, and he relaxed as the warm colour again crept into his cheeks.

'Oh, Anne, I . . .'

He leaned forward and kissed her briefly and rather clumsily, then stood up as her father's heavy measured tread sounded in the corridor.

'We'd better arrange it with your parents at once. I leave for America in two weeks, and I want us to marry and for you to be in Elvan Hall, before I go. Can you manage it so soon?'

Anne nodded rather wryly. She already had a trousseau collected.

'I'll manage . . . Francis,' she said, the name sounding strange to her lips.

'Let's tell your parents, then,' he said eagerly, as the door opened. 'We must have their approval, mustn't we, Anne?'

But what of Mrs. Wyatt's approval? wondered Anne, seeing the first rocks ahead on her new journey. What of that?

★ ★ ★

Stephen Drummond was adamant. There would be no wedding arranged at such short notice. If they were seriously in love, then there was no need for such hurry, and the love would bind them together until Francis came back from America and a proper wedding could be arranged.

His sharp eyes sought Anne's when he mentioned love and she turned away, glancing quickly at Francis whose face was impassive.

Anne's pleading eyes went to her mother, and Mrs. Drummond looked at them both with concern.

'Are you sure, darling?' she asked Anne. 'It's very sudden, Mr. Wyatt . . . Francis.'

'We're sure,' said Anne, going to stand beside Francis.

'You mean that the real reason behind your break-up with Graham was that you had fallen in love with . . . er . . . Francis?'

Anne's face went scarlet and this time she avoided looking at Francis entirely. How could she answer this but by the truth?

'Something like that,' she said, in a low voice, and felt his fingers tighten on her arm. 'Francis has reasons why he wants us to marry before he leaves for America.'

'If I can see you privately, sir,' he said to Stephen Drummond, 'I can go into my affairs, and I think I can assure you that Anne will be taken care of.'

The sharp eyes were now on Francis.

'Very well, come into my study. No doubt my wife and Anne will wish to prepare a meal?'

'Of course,' said Nell Drummond hastily. 'Er . . . perhaps you would like to stay the night if we have further things to discuss, Francis?'

He smiled gently, and Anne thought how young he could look at times.

'Thank you, but I must return to my flat in Carlisle. I have much to do before leaving, but I'd like to return in a few days. Anne and I have some shopping to do for two rings . . . that is, if my talk with Mr. Drummond is satisfactory.'

'Better not keep him waiting, then,' advised Mrs. Drummond.

In the kitchen there was silence between the two women while Anne set out cups and saucers on a large tray.

'It's true then,' her mother said at length. 'You broke with Graham because you fell in love with someone else?'

Anne nodded.

'Graham guessed, but really, Mummy, he wanted out of it, too. We only went along with it while we were young, to please all of you. Now we're older we want to choose for ourselves. Thank goodness we had the courage to stop in time.'

'And you chose Mr. Wyatt? Did he declare his love for you before you left Wyatt's?'

This time Anne's face flamed.

'Mummy, I . . . I . . . '

'I'm asking too many questions?'

'No. It's just that . . .'

She hesitated. If she confessed to her mother that Francis had not declared his love, she would immediately try to persuade her out of such a marriage. And perhaps she would be right, thought Anne, rather disconsolately. Would her own love really be enough for both? Wasn't she being rather a fool?

'It's all right, darling, I won't pry any more. You're old enough now to make up your own mind. I suppose we ought to have champagne, but the most we ever seem to manage here is the odd bottle of sherry, and some home-made wines gifted by people in the parish. Some of them are most potent, too, as your father and I have discovered.'

Mrs. Drummond was moving bottles about in a large store cupboard.

'Ah, here we are — Celebration Cream. This should do, shouldn't it, darling? I remember now that I started laying in a few bottles against more people calling with presents as we were using all the rest up ... Oh!' She looked at Anne levelly. 'People will talk, dear.'

'Surely you and Daddy can stand more talk. They've all talked their heads off already when Graham and I called it off. It's my life, after all, not other people's.'

'Of course, my dear.'

Her mother came to hug her, and Anne swallowed hard to control the rush of tears to her eyes, then she picked up her tray of crockery. She was going to marry Francis Wyatt. He would belong to no one else but herself, and surely there could be no greater happiness than sharing the life of the man one loved.

'Bring the sherry, Mummy,' she said. 'Let's have something special for tea, too. I can hear Daddy and Francis, and there are no raised voices, so it must be all right!'

2

At the small church she had known all her life, Anne Drummond became Mrs. Francis Wyatt, with only a few close friends to witness the ceremony, even if the whole of Arndale had turned out, either to wish her well or to get a good look at the bridegroom. Graham had, unfortunately, gone to Norway on holiday, or he would, Anne was sure, have been delighted to have come to the ceremony.

Mrs. Wyatt had sent her regrets and had said that she was unwell and Helen would be required to help her over her illness. Judith was much too young to travel to Scotland on her own.

Francis had gone white.

'I expected this,' he told Anne. 'Do you mind that my . . . my people won't be at the wedding?'

'I don't know,' said Anne frankly. 'My

parents will mind, but I don't think I blame your mother. After all, I've been rather sprung on her, haven't I?'

Again the hard look came over Francis' face.

'I did what I believed to be necessary,' he told her, rather curtly.

Mrs. Drummond had showed her concern.

'You've met Mrs. Wyatt?' she asked Anne. 'At the office, I believe.'

'I have.'

'It seems strange that Francis hasn't taken you home to Elvan Hall, but wants to take you there for the first time as his bride.'

Anne had also thought it strange, but she did not wish to show that to her mother.

'I think he's romantic,' she said lightly, and saw by her mother's small smile that this had been the right touch.

'Don't let . . . anyone . . . try to bully you, my dear,' she warned, however. 'If you've any battles to fight, just remember you're your father's daughter, and have a good share of his courage in you.'

'And my mother's,' said Anne softly.

'And your mother's,' agreed Mrs. Drummond, her eyes twinkling.

Anne and Francis had spent a very brief honeymoon at New Abbey, where Francis wanted to explore the ruins of Sweetheart Abbey. He had shown Anne a great deal of gentleness and consideration, and though she had sighed a little in her secret heart for the love which might have been, she was happy.

Three days before Francis was due to leave for America, they travelled southwest again, through Carlisle, and then into Cumberland towards Cockermouth.

'How beautiful it is,' said Anne, looking at the freshness of the countryside and the distant mountains of the Lake District.

'Wait till you see Elvan Hall,' said Francis, as the car left the main road and they snaked along through narrow hill roads, passing small farms and picturesque cottages, till a beautiful silvery river could be seen winding its way along the valley. Francis stopped the car and they looked down on an ancient grey-stone house, which seemed to grow out of fine parkland. It was sheltered by beech trees to the west, and masses of rhododendrons and azaleas to the east.

'In spring the woods are full of snowdrops and aconites, then crocuses and daffodils with primroses and violets.'

'You love spring best of all?'

'I love every season in turn, but spring seems to me a time of re-birth, and hope, and a belief in all eternal things. It's only just past, and this year . . . this year, perhaps, it has all come true.'

Anne saw his eyes on her, and caught her breath. For a moment it almost seemed as though he really did care for her, then the moment was gone, and he was climbing back into the car.

'I'm sure you'll come to love it,

Anne,' he told her happily. 'I saw your face when you first looked down on the house.'

Anne nodded. She had felt her heart contract at the beauty of the old place, and it must have shown on her face. Was that why Francis had looked at her with love? Could she only reach his heart through Elvan Hall, and not by being herself?

Anne was silent as they drove the two miles to the large, beautiful wrought-iron gates, and Francis drove through, the car wheels crunching on the gravel as it swung up to the wide doors.

Anne got out, feeling suddenly cold with nerves, unhelped by the white look which was again on Francis' face, as an elderly woman came out to welcome them.

'This is Mrs. Hansett, our house-keeper,' he introduced. 'This is my wife, Jessie.'

'How do you do, ma'am,' said Mrs. Hansett politely, as Anne shook her hand.

'Where is my mother?' Francis was asking. 'Will you get Tom to remove our cases?'

'The mistress is in bed, Mr. Francis. She hasn't been well. Miss Judith is with her, and Miss Helen is over at Cravenhill.'

'I see. Why isn't Judith at school? It isn't end of term yet.'

'She's had measles, sir. She was sent home last Wednesday.'

'I see,' he said again.

Francis took Anne's hand as they mounted the wide steps to the terrace, then almost grimly he swept her into his arms.

'The Wyatt brides are traditionally carried over the threshold,' he told her, rather harshly. 'That goes for you too, Anne.'

He carried her as though she weighed much less than her hundred and twenty pounds, then set her down on a Persian rug which covered a large part of the polished wood floor in the spacious hall.

The new mistress of Elvan Hall had come home.

* * *

Penelope Wyatt lay in bed surrounded by magazines, while a small, thin pale girl sat on a chair beside her, disentangling a ball of wool. The little girl looked up with large, rather frightened eyes as Francis showed Anne into the luxuriously furnished bedroom quite out of keeping with the house, after a brief knock on the door.

Mrs. Wyatt looked even more fluffy, clad in a dressing jacket in palest pink, trimmed with white swansdown. The soft furnishings were also of pale pink, the paintwork white, with a beautiful soft dove-grey carpet on the floor. The pinks succeeded in creating a sugary effect, the first jarring note Anne had found in the truly beautiful old house.

Francis had briefly shown her the main rooms downstairs, but he had promised her a full tour of inspection after she had met his mother and sister, and rested a little after her journey. Already Jessie Hansett had gone to prepare a light appetising meal for both of them.

Although they had met before, Mrs. Wyatt gave no sign of ever having seen Anne in her life.

'You must forgive me if I have done little to make you welcome, Miss . . . ah . . . My son has rather sprung his marriage on his family. The haste seemed to me rather . . . indecent, Francis. Not in keeping with Elvan Hall.'

'I felt it was necessary, Mother,' said Francis, and Anne could feel the undercurrents between the two. His eyes had met those of his mother's defiantly, as though swords had been crossed, and Anne could feel his fingers gripping her shoulder. Just where did she stand between the two? she wondered uneasily.

'And you're one of Francis's employees? A typist, I understand.'

Anne flushed and her chin lifted.

'I *was* his private secretary,' she said evenly. 'We've known each other for two years.'

Mrs. Wyatt gathered her magazines together as though Anne hadn't spoken.

'Take these downstairs, child,' she said to Judith, having caught the little girl smiling shyly to Anne.

'Are your measles better?' Anne asked, smiling in return.

'Yes, thanks.'

'Spots all gone? I had measles, too, at your age.'

'I meant *now*, Judith,' broke in Mrs. Wyatt coldly. 'Now! Are you deaf, child? Tell Mrs. Hansett you'll have tea up here with me.'

The little girl's disappointment showed in her eyes as she turned uncertainly to Francis, who suddenly put an arm round her and ruffled her mop of straight dark hair.

'We'll talk later, love,' he promised her. 'I've got that lovely book on wild flowers you wanted. It's in my case.'

'Oh, Francis!' cried Judith, hugging him round the waist.

Anne's eyes were soft as she watched. This was the Francis Wyatt she loved, this gentle considerate man on whom she felt she could depend utterly. Then her eyes turned to the woman on the bed, her heart quailing when she saw the anger betrayed on her round, plump, childish face.

'Must I have my wishes entirely disegarded?' she was saying petulantly, and Judith quickly picked up the magazines and hurried to the door. As she turned, Anne could see a closed look on her face, such as she had seen on Francis'. Already she could feel the strength of personality of this soft-looking, frilly woman who was their mother.

But people had a right to grow and develop according to their own person-alities, thought Anne rather fiercely. Could it be that Francis had no real deep love to give her, because at some time in his life it had become submerged, then stunted by sheer neglect? Was the same thing, even now, beginning in Judith?

Anne looked at their mother, but decided she could not judge while the older woman was so angry. She rose to her feet, realising that her first interview with her new mother-in-law was at an end, and as their eyes met, she also knew that it was war between them.

But Anne felt strength in her limbs as she drew herself up to her full height, unaware that her beauty had a quality which far outshone the prettiness which Penelope Wyatt had had in her heyday.

Francis and Judith both needed room to grow, even in such a spacious home as Elvan Hall, and Anne was going to fight fiercely to give them that right.

'I'm sorry to be indisposed and can't show you my home,' Mrs. Wyatt was saying, rather tonelessly, to Anne. 'No doubt Francis can take my place.'

'Anne is eager to see *our* home,' Francis put in smoothly, though again she could feel his fingers gripping her arm. 'I'm sure she'll love it as I do, since it will be hers for the rest of her life. I presume the plans for redecoration and renovation are still on my desk?'

'No, I have them,' Mrs. Wyatt said flatly. 'There are changes I would like to make. I told you so before, Francis.'

'Changes can only be made with my permission,' Francis told her, the angry colour high in his cheeks.

Mrs. Wyatt changed her tactics, as she suddenly groped for a handkerchief and put it to her eyes.

'It was my home before you were born,' she said thickly. 'Now you come here with a . . . a strange young woman all ready to oust me. How can you do such a thing at such short notice, Francis? Surely I should know by now what is best for the Hall.'

The white closed look was back on his face.

'We'll discuss it later, Mother. Come, Anne.'

'Good afternoon, Mrs. Wyatt,' said Anne politely but only received a sniff in reply.

As they walked back downstairs, she could feel the anger and tension still in Francis.

'Go on into the drawing room, Anne . . . along there and through that door. I'll join you in a moment. There's some mail on my desk, I believe.'

'All right, Francis,' she agreed, then on impulse caught his arm. 'Don't worry. We have each other, haven't we?'

He stared at her, his eyes still remote, then he relaxed.

'Bless you, Anne. Of course we have.'

Anne walked along the broad, softly carpeted corridor at the foot of the stairs towards the drawing room, pausing as she heard a girl's flute-like voice coming to her clearly through the slightly open door.

'She's a pretty young lady, Helen.'

'That makes it all the worse. I *told* Francis that the only way to get Mother to accept Caroline was to bring home someone even less suitable, but the nitwit goes and marries her! I only told him in fun, too, and I didn't think he was paying any attention. How could he be such a fool! He does the strangest things . . . '

Anne felt as though she was rooted to the carpet, the words falling on her head like blows. Who was Caroline? Was it someone Francis had loved, and of whom his mother had disapproved?

'Someone even less suitable,' she repeated.

She was obviously that someone . . . a typist . . . an employee . . .

Yet Francis *had* married her. Why?

She wanted to run back along the corridor and find somewhere she could be alone, even for a little while. Her head was whirring, and she didn't want to meet this other sister of Francis's, this girl with the pretty flute-like voice, who seemed to be his adviser with regard to his love affairs at any rate.

Anne turned, then saw Mrs. Hansett

hurrying towards her.

'Do you want the drawing room, ma'am?' she was asking, though Anne felt the warm colour flooding her own checks. The housekeeper, she suspected, was aware that she had been listening outside the door.

'Yes, please,' she said, as evenly as she could.

'In here, then.'

Mrs. Hansett held the door open and Anne stepped into the large room which was again well-carpeted, with chintz-covered chairs and sofas drawn up round a huge log fire. The walls were dark and richly carved in panelled wood, and there were many paintings in heavy ornate gold-painted frames. From the centre of the room hung a huge crystal chandelier which Anne viewed with respect, recognising that it was quartz crystal.

A tall slender girl with the same pretty childish features as her mother, but dainty and elegant in a young girl, rose languidly to her feet. Anne could see that her skin was warmly coloured, as though she spent many hours in the fresh air. Little Judith had also stood up, and was smiling at Anne, shyly.

'This is Miss Helen, ma'am,' the housekeeper was introducing. 'She was out when you arrived. The new mistress . . . Mrs. Francis.'

'Hello there,' drawled Helen Wyatt. 'You're a surprise. Anne, isn't it?'

'Yes . . . Anne. So I believe,' said Anne, managing to look directly at her older sister-in-law. 'How do you do, Helen?'

'How do you do.'

'I'll just bring tea in now,' Mrs. Hansett was saying. 'You're going upstairs, Miss Judith.'

'Yes, Jessie.'

'She isn't going to serve you with a tray of poison,' Helen admonished her. 'Someone must keep Mummy company.'

Why? Wondered Anne, though she said nothing.

'Do you like your new abode?' Helen was asking. 'Think it makes it all worth while?'

'I don't know what you mean,' Anne told her rather stiffly.

'No? I guess you must love Francis, then.'

Anne was about to assure her, rather defiantly, that she did when she remembered the remarks she had overheard.

What had they meant? Would she begin to understand her strange marriage to Francis Wyatt when she met a girl called Caroline? But if he really loved Caroline, why had he married her?

Anne felt an odd wave of fear and loneliness. She was mistress of this great house, but she felt alien, suddenly, to every part of it. She had no business here, she thought, trying hard to still the fear in her heart.

Then the door opened and Francis walked in.

'So you've met my wife, Helen,' he

said, with a smile as he came forward to warm his hands in front of the fire. 'Good. I hope you two will be friends.'

'Oh, darling,' said Helen, with a laugh, 'you do the strangest things and expect us all to applaud. Poor Anne must feel like a fish out of water.'

'You can soon put that right,' said Francis sharply.

'Give us time. You spring a new bride on us . . . a new mistress of the house . . . and we have all to adjust in a moment.'

'Why not?' asked Francis. 'You knew I planned to marry.'

'But not . . . '

Helen bit her lip and had the grace to colour deeply.

But not me, thought Anne.

They were saved from further discussion by the arrival of Mrs. Hansett with a heavy wooden trolley. Anne felt that her appetite had deserted her, but once again Francis had put his long sensitive hands on her shoulders.

'You pour, Anne,' he said gently. 'You must be hungry, dear. Jessie has made a special effort for you, too.'

This time Jessie Hansett's smile for her was completely natural.

'It's an occasion, ma'am. It's lovely to have a new bride at Elvan Hall.'

Warmth slid into Anne's heart.

'Thank you, Mrs. Hansett,' she said huskily.

* * *

There was much to do in the two days before Francis left for America. He conducted Anne carefully all over the old house, carrying a folder containing plans and suggestions worked out by a firm of interior decorators. Anne had studied the plans carefully and thought that the suggestions made were excellent, though Francis had written in several notes of caution regarding parts of the house which must be carefully preserved without alteration in any way.

'These notes aren't enough either,

Anne,' he told her. 'As you see, many things have become neglected. Tapestries require to be repaired, and I would like to preserve some old hangings which have been embroidered.'

'I couldn't tackle those jobs,' said Anne quickly. 'I'm no needlewoman, Francis.'

'I don't expect that of you,' he returned smoothly. 'I would expect you to employ a skilled needlewoman. In fact . . .'

He paused, rubbing his cheek thoughtfully.

'Have you someone in mind?'

He turned to her, almost with a start.

'No,' he said, flatly, 'no one. I shall leave all that to you, my dear. You can perhaps arrange for someone to come from London. I'm making financial arrangements for you so that you may spend as you wish, though I know it will be used carefully and judiciously.'

They had mounted a broad stairway of polished wood, blackened with age.

'You like it, Anne?' he asked eagerly, catching her hand.

'It's very beautiful,' said Anne truthfully.

But how could she ever think of it all as hers?

'I knew you were right for it,' Francis told her, his voice deepening, and suddenly his arms were round her, drawing her close.

Anne's heart raced, but even as she felt his nearness, she remembered that he only cared for her because it had become necessary for him to marry, and in his opinion she had been his most suitable choice.

She forgot her resolve that her own love would be enough for both of them, and stiffened a little in his arms. Immediately he let her go.

'I'm sorry,' he told her, rather stiffly. 'I forgot that there are certain things about our marriage I must respect.'

'Such as?'

'Your right to your own feelings,' he told her roughly, and she was silent.

Had he guessed her feelings?

Colouring, she walked ahead of him. 'We have very little time, Francis. Shall we check the bedrooms?'

Their own bedroom was a huge place as different from Mrs. Wyatt's as possible.

'It hasn't been changed over many years,' Francis told her. 'It was my father's and grandfather's. Mother never cared for it, so she chose her own further down the corridor.'

'I see there's little to be done to it, from your report here,' said Anne, leafing over the pages.

'I thought it unnecessary,' said Francis.

'Nevertheless, I would like to make one or two small changes,' said Anne, her chin firming a little. She had no idea why she was asserting herself in this way. In its own way the bedroom was perfect, but it had rather sombre overtones, not in keeping with a happily married young couple. 'That is, unless you'd prefer me, too, to choose another bedroom further down the corridor.'

Their gazes locked and she saw Francis turn white.

'You must do as you wish,' he said stiffly. 'You are mistress here. You are entitled to your own wishes over the matter of . . . of a bedroom.'

It was a hollow victory. Anne inclined her head, feeling that she had gained nothing and feeling, too, that she had somehow hurt Francis. But she didn't know what to say to put things right between them.

'I take it the girls have been allowed their own choice with regard to their rooms?'

'Certainly. This is one of our guest bedrooms. There are three more on this floor. We've turned part of the top floor into a flat for the Hansetts, Tom and Jessie.'

'I'm glad of that,' smiled Anne, with relief. She had quite enough to digest at the moment. 'I take it that they, too, are happy with their own decorations?'

'They were all freshly done two years ago when the gardener's cottage was condemned. It hadn't been built to stand the test of time, as has the Hall,' said Francis rather dryly.

'And they like the flat?'

'It's warm and comfortable . . . and convenient. They can use the back stairs to the kitchen. I've asked Tom to show you over the gardens when I go. It isn't so difficult to keep as it looks, with a good rotary mower and well laid out beds and shrubberies. Besides, the ground round the house has been much reduced. We let the park and fields beyond for pasture land. My sister also breeds young horses and Shetland ponies. She has the use of all the stables, and pasture lands to the west of the house.'

'She's very young for that, isn't she?'

'She's been riding since she was a baby.' Suddenly he smiled. 'I'm sure Helen will be happy to show you the ponies. They are the great love of her life.'

'I'd like that,' said Anne, rather shyly, and he took her hand again.

'I know it isn't easy for you, dear, but you have my . . . my gratitude for all you are doing.'

But she didn't want his gratitude, thought Anne forlornly, as they walked back down the polished stairs with the red carpeting running down the middle. She wanted his love. How different it would all be if they could claim stewardship of it together.

'And remember, you mustn't let my mother overrule you,' he told her firmly. 'She . . . she has her own ideas, ideas which my father was at great pains to modify. She mustn't be allowed to order improvements which are not in keeping with the house.'

Anne said nothing. Soon she would be on her own, after Francis went. However would she manage to keep Mrs. Wyatt from giving whatever orders she wished in her own home?

Not hers . . . mine, thought Anne. My own house.

But it wasn't hers. It was alien to her. Even Francis was sometimes alien to her. What had she done? wondered Anne, as her feet again sank into soft carpeting. She was greatly afraid that the road she had chosen was far too full of potholes . . .

3

'Would you like me to come with you to the airport?' Anne asked, trying not to betray her feeling of depression with loneliness at his departure. While he was with her, his presence gave her authority, and there had been a strange inward happiness at having him so close to her, even if it had been bitter-sweet.

But now he was going and there would only be herself, Helen and Mrs. Wyatt left in the house, besides the Hansetts, Judith having been obliged to return to school.

The little girl had shyly held Anne's hand.

'I'm glad you've come,' she whispered. 'I like having you here, although I like Caroline, too.'

Anne had resisted the temptation to question the child. Who was Caroline, and what did she mean to Francis? She also resisted the temptation to question Francis, feeling that he had enough on his mind.

Anne had been able to do little for him, as he preferred to do his own packing, and Miss Dalton was arranging all the relevant papers for him to take with him. Anne recognised that Louise Dalton was a better secretary than she had ever been, and felt rather humble when she saw how efficiently everything was arranged.

But she was now Francis' wife, not his secretary, and that task was even more Herculean, she thought despondently, as she looked behind her at the large old house which was going to be left in her charge, and possibly two other women to fight for full authority.

Mrs. Wyatt had decided to come downstairs to see Francis away, clad in rich warm furs, though the day was warm and sunny.

Tom Hansett had recently cut the huge lawns and the herbaceous borders were full of colour with peonies,

Californian poppies, blue and purple iris, and a variety of small colourful plants. The huge, rather overgrown rhododendrons and azaleas formed a windbreak for the house, and Anne looked round at the peaceful scene, the warm fresh air blowing her hair, while the river, fast-flowing with clear, pure unpolluted water, made a soft surging sound behind the call of the birds.

It was beautiful, thought Anne, a strange new intensity of feeling taking hold of her heart. So had many mistresses of Elvan Hall stood on the broad steps taking leave of the master, no doubt many of them riding into war and facing unknown dangers. So had other women before her been left to guard the heritage while their menfolk helped to preserve peace in the land.

She saw Francis' eyes on her, as he put the last of his belongings into the car. He had kissed his mother and sister with a whispered word that he was leaving his wife in their care, and now he turned to Anne, kissing her too, rather clumsily.

'Look after . . . ' he paused, then said, deliberately, 'Look after *yourself*, Anne. I hope I shan't be away more than two or three weeks.'

It was a lifetime to Anne, then she caught sight of a gleam of amusement in Helen's eyes. Francis had said a warm goodbye, but it hadn't been the poignant leavetaking of a young husband for a new bride.

'I don't care,' thought Anne, defiantly tossing back her heavy fair hair. 'It was precious to me . . . and to Francis.'

She fought back the tears as she waved him away, knowing that they would put her at a disadvantage when she faced the women on her own. They had talked a great deal, to each other and to Francis, but she had scarcely listened to their chatter. Now the silence seemed absolute, as all three stood on the steps, with Jessie Hansett in the doorway, and Tom already making his way back to the gardens.

'Jessie, I shall want you in my room after tea,' Mrs. Wyatt was saying. 'There are several things I wish to discuss with you.'

Ignoring Anne entirely, she walked heavily back into the house. Helen walked forward quickly and took her mother's arm, throwing a glance at Anne over her shoulder.

Anne was left on the steps alone, and as she walked back inside, she knew that her own particular war had started. This time the mistress of Elvan was at war, not the master!

* * *

It was obvious to Anne, very soon after Francis' departure, that Mrs. Wyatt was choosing to ignore her presence in the house. She asked Mrs. Hansett to come to her room every morning to receive orders, and meals were silent affairs, with only Helen to make the occasional remark.

At first Anne felt hurt and bruised,

her heart aching for Francis more than she would have believed possible. She had not realised how much it was coming to mean to her to have his constant companionship.

Mrs. Hansett was obviously ill at ease in her presence, occasionally looking as though she wanted to pass some remark, then turning away abruptly. Helen came in and out at odd hours, and although Anne knew that she was in charge of the horses and ponies, she had little idea what that involved, and didn't feel like asking Helen to take her round. Francis' sister was wayward towards her, occasionally greeting her in a friendly way, then becoming coolly withdrawn as though she was remembering that Anne was supposed to be in Coventry.

Anne felt too confused at first to know what to do about this state of affairs. Now that Francis had gone, she felt too much of an intruder to assert herself. Then one morning Mrs.

Hansett asked if she might speak with her privately.

'Of course,' smiled Anne, rising from the breakfast table where she was enjoying an extra cup of coffee. Helen was already on her way to the stables, and Mrs. Wyatt was having breakfast in bed.

'What can I do for you, Mrs. Hansett?'

'It's . . . er . . . it's the bills, ma'am. It's the month end and Mrs. Wyatt says you'll be paying them now. I've got a note of all the housekeeping bills for the month and . . . and . . .'

She stopped, confused, and Anne's brows wrinkled. Then suddenly her head began to clear, and it seemed as though she was able to think for the first time since Francis left.

But of course! There was the matter of accounts to be paid, and wages, and the ordering of supplies. Francis had given her full instructions and had arranged a bank account for her.

'Come with me to the study, Mrs.

71

Hansett,' she said crisply, and the housekeeper followed her almost eagerly.

Anne sat down at Francis' desk, and motioned Mrs. Hansett to sit down.

'I understand that I pay your salary as well as the bills,' she said with a smile, and saw the older woman's eyes clear with relief.

'Yes, ma'am, there are several wages to be paid today. Mr. Wyatt used to get the money from the bank, but he said you would pay by cheque. I . . . I don't think it's a good thing for a young lady like you to be carrying a lot of money from the bank.'

'And you all find a cheque quite agreeable to you?'

'Oh yes, ma'am. We can get our own money.'

'Give me the bills and I shall write the cheques this morning. If you call in with a cup of coffee, say . . . in an hour's time . . . I shall have your cheques ready, and I will also have gone into these bills. I should like to see them before I write out the cheques.'

'Yes, ma'am,' said Mrs. Hansett, with respect.

'Oh, and as I'm paying the bills, Mrs. Hansett, I think I ought to take over the running of the Hall, especially since Mrs. Wyatt is not keeping so well, and Miss Helen already has a job to do. I . . . er . . . ' Her heart quailed a little. 'It's what Mr. Francis wished, and I'd better have a word with Mrs. Wyatt and . . . ah . . . tell her that I'm willing to take this responsibility off her shoulders.'

This time the gleam of approval became a warm smile.

'Very well, ma'am.'

'Though I'll need advice over the housekeeping, Mrs. Hansett,' said Anne quickly, feeling nervous again at the thought of the task ahead.

'I'll be happy to help in any way I can. Mr. Francis asked me to give you my support before he left and I promised.'

'Oh,' said Anne, her warm glow

receding a little. So Mrs. Hansett had decided to stand by her, not for her own sake, but for Francis'. Still, it was better than having to fight everybody.

'Very well, Mrs. Hansett,' she said, nodding dismissal.

An hour later she had gone through the household accounts, writing out cheques, but feeling rather appalled by the amount of money being spent on items which, she felt, could be cut down with no loss of comfort.

She paid the staff their wages, smiling pleasantly but with authority, then drank her coffee thoughtfully. Mrs. Wyatt didn't make her appearance until lunch time and Anne glanced at her watch.

Mrs. Wyatt seemed to have little objection to holding court from her bed. There were things to be ironed out between them, and Anne rose briskly to her feet. It was never any good putting off unpleasant tasks, and she quickly made her way out into the corridor and up the broad main staircase.

Mrs. Wyatt's voice sounded quite cheerful when she shouted for Anne to come in, in answer to her firm knock. Her face grew cool, however, when she recognised her visitor.

'Oh, it's you!'

'I'm sorry to interrupt the privacy of your bedroom, Mrs. Wyatt,' said Anne, pleasantly but purposefully. 'However, I feel that we have matters of some urgency to discuss, so I took the liberty of coming to you. I hope you're feeling better this morning?'

Mrs. Wyatt merely inclined her head in answer to the query about her health. She adjusted her fluffy wrap on her shoulders.

'I can't imagine what these matters of urgency could be,' she commented.

Anne produced the household bills, together with pencil and paper, on which she had jotted a few notes.

'These bills, Mrs. Wyatt.'

'They don't concern me any more. My son is master of this house. As his wife, *you* are responsible for the household accounts, and it's your duty to pay those bills. They're not my responsibility.'

'I agree,' said Anne smoothly. 'I'm glad you recognise that arrangement. However, since I'm paying the bills, I think it's only fair that I should also order our supplies. I find much in these bills very wasteful. It should cost a great deal less to feed this household, even allowing for entertaining.'

Mrs. Wyatt regarded her balefully.

'I shouldn't go out of your way to advertise the fact that you've been brought up in ... ah ... rather different circumstances from those you now enjoy,' she said softly. 'I'm quite capable of ordering what we need, and if you're wise you'll leave that to me, since you lack experience and may find it difficult. It's sufficient for you to write the cheques at the end of the month.'

Anne had flushed scarlet at Mrs. Wyatt's reference to her own background, and for a moment she quailed a little. Then her chin lifted. Allowing for luxury such as she little knew, and also for lavish hospitality, the bills were still too high, and a visit to the kitchens had confirmed Anne's belief that rather more common sense could be applied. She had a feeling that Mrs. Hansett would appreciate firmer control, rather than otherwise.

'I abhor waste,' she said quietly, 'like many others of my background. I'm sorry I can't agree that you should continue to order our food while I pay for it . . . blindly, if I may put it like that. Perhaps my experience is nil, but how can I learn if I don't take responsibility?'

'Surely it's enough that Francis should bring us a girl like you . . . out of the blue . . . even more unsuitable than . . .'

Mrs. Wyatt's burst of anger broke off abruptly, and she bit her lip.

'Very well,' she said. 'Make a fool of yourself, and of him. You're entirely unfitted to be here. My son always showed lack of judgement in his personal life. I . . . I suppose we can be grateful that he has the ability to run his business more efficiently.'

'That certainly ought to be a comfort to you,' returned Anne. Francis had told her that his mother was entirely dependent on him, and his sisters till they were of age, though Helen was pulling her weight by working as his groom. Anne knew, too, from her position as his secretary, that the wealth and prosperity of the company was increasing, and had done since his father died. They had every reason to be grateful to Francis. Mrs. Wyatt should be so proud of him, instead of criticising him.

Then Anne's gaze softened a little. Perhaps she *was* proud of him, so proud that, inversely, she didn't dare show it. Could that be her main reason for resenting Anne, and in fact, for thinking that nobody was good enough for Francis, not even the girl Helen had mentioned?

Anne considered a little as she rose to

go, still firm in her resolution to take charge of running Elvan Hall.

'Please don't let's be bad friends,' she said gently. 'I know it must be hard on you to have me foisted on to you, but Francis wanted a quick wedding, or I'd have preferred to have you get to know me first. But we *are* married now, and I've got to live here a very long time. All my life, in fact. Surely it would make it easier for both of us if we pulled together, and not against each other.'

But the older woman's expression showed no sign of softening, and Anne knew that she might just as well have saved her breath.

'All your life?' she repeated. 'My, that *is* a long time. I hope you settle down then. Others . . . others before you have found themselves being rejected by Elvan. The house didn't like them . . . or something. It takes a very special woman to fit in. That's why . . . ' Again she broke off, shrugging.

'I can't even talk to you,' she said,

with a wave of dismissal. 'I don't think we even talk the same language.'

Again Anne flushed. The soft Scots accent was noticeable in her speech, though Francis had not found it irritating. But of course, Mrs. Wyatt might have been speaking figuratively.

'Send Mrs. Hansett up to me,' she commanded, 'and see that the door is shut properly when you leave.'

Controlling her anger, Anne collected her papers, and walked quickly across the room, feeling the older woman's eyes almost burning a hole in her back.

'She hates me,' thought Anne, feeling rather sick. No one had ever shown such hatred towards her, ever before.

Her new home was one which was beginning to envelop her with hatred, and not with love. She didn't even have the true love of a man for his new bride.

★   ★   ★

Mrs. Hansett began coming to Anne each morning to discuss any problems which came up regarding the running of the house. Anne found that she had to make decisions and sometimes she made them with outward authority, but inwardly praying that they were right.

When it was the wrong decision, Mrs. Wyatt was never slow to make a cutting comment and Anne's ready colour would warm her cheeks, but she learned by her mistakes, and gained confidence as the days slowly passed.

Occasionally she received a letter from Francis, little different from the crisp, business letters he used to dictate to her, but she cherished them as a link with him, and she was proud to feel that he was handling his business affairs successfully. He also hoped that Anne would be feeling at home, now, and would have had time to study the plans for renovation and redecoration.

Anne had rather laid those plans to one side, feeling vaguely disturbed by them, yet strangely attracted, too, rather like a kitten eyeing a wasps' nest, she thought, with a smile. Or could it even be a hornet's? she wondered, catching Mrs. Wyatt's eye one day as she found herself a comfortable seat by the fire and began to study the plans. The work for the bedrooms had already been put in hand for the following week.

'Some of those lovely old tapestries and chair covers could be repaired carefully,' said Anne to Helen an hour later, when the other girl called in for a cup of coffee.

'You know, I read somewhere that the museums employ women . . . at least, I suppose it would be women . . . to repair old and precious embroidered articles. I think it's possible to take a degree in that sort of thing at university. Perhaps it would be possible to employ someone to come here and put all our own precious hangings into good repair.'

Helen was looking at her sideways, her eyes gleaming.

'Well, my dear Anne, you won't really

have far to look. Caroline Cook has just qualified, and is in fact, going to Goldsmith's in London in September, but I'm sure she would come here first of all . . . if you asked her nicely.'

Anne said nothing for a moment, gazing at Helen's impassive face. There had been nothing in her words but a desire to be helpful, yet the light casual tones had only been overtones, and Helen was looking at her with a gleam in her eye. Mrs. Wyatt had flushed.

'I'm quite sure there's no need to bother Caroline Cook,' she said firmly, 'especially now!'

'No, you never really encouraged her, did you, Mother?' asked Helen. 'Don't you think that was a mistake . . . from *your* point of view, I mean?'

'A mistake?' asked Anne.

'Of course. Things could have been put right ages ago. I refer, of course, to the tapestries.'

Mrs. Wyatt was glaring at her daughter.

'Who is this girl?' asked Anne,

determined to know more. The name teased her memory, but she knew she had never met anyone by that name who could do embroidery.

'She's the sister of Ronald Cook at Cravenhill, a small farm which the family have rented from us for generations. Ronald and his wife, Beatrice, run the farm now, but Caroline took after her grandmother . . . ' she shot a gleaming look at her mother, ' . . . and was an excellent needlewoman.'

'That will do, Helen,' said Mrs. Wyatt.

'Well, she is excellent. Luckily her mother had the sense to allow her to go and train or she . . . she'd be spending her days feeding the hens and collecting eggs. At least Ronald allowed her to keep on with the course after Mrs. Cook died.'

'You like this girl?' asked Anne impulsively, and with sudden insight.

'I love her,' said Helen simply. 'She's older than me, but she's my best friend. We used to play together when we were children, then I wasn't allowed to play at the farm any more.'

'Tom Cook wasn't so particular a farmer as his son Ronald,' said Mrs. Wyatt sharply. 'Ronald at least keeps the place clean. You used to come home in a disgusting state . . . '

'Well, we had fun,' said Helen defiantly.

In that moment Helen looked less like her mother than Anne had ever seen her, and she began to suspect there might be a lot of her father in the girl. It was evident in her outdoor look. Mrs. Wyatt looked much more like an indoor plant.

'She . . . Caroline . . . wasn't good enough, was she, Mother?' asked Helen, her eyes gleaming again. 'To play with me, I mean?'

'But is she good enough to do the embroidery?' asked Anne, deciding that it was time to finish with past grievances.

'None better,' Helen assured her.

'Then I shall call and see her,' Anne

85

decided, making a note of the girl's name and address. 'I'd better telephone first. But I would like to see samples of her work and it would be better for me to go to her.'

'I shan't be a party to your employing Caroline Cook,' said Mrs. Wyatt flatly.

Anne blinked. Surely if the girl was available, and could do the job, it didn't matter if Helen had long ago come home smelling of the farmyard after a good day's play with another girl! Now she saw the look of hope on the other girl's face. If Caroline was her best friend, surely it should give Helen a lot of pleasure having her here to work for a month or two.

'I think the main thing is her skill,' said Anne quietly. 'It seems to me that we're very fortunate to have someone qualified on our own doorstep, as it were.'

'You're a stupid girl,' Mrs. Wyatt told her. 'You see nothing else worthy of consideration but the obvious. It never occurs to you that things here are not so simple as they appear. However, in regard to the tapestries and all the other things which require to be repaired and restored, I have no choice but to leave it to you. I would like, however, to see the decorators before they start on the drawing room. Henry, Francis' father, promised me that I could have my choice next time that room was done. He supervised the last plans and I find the effect too dark. There's no need to live in a dark world these days. Today there is such a wide choice of colour, whereas at one time everything had to be dark brown.'

Anne nodded. For once she was in agreement with the older woman, remembering the old Manse at home which had looked very gloomy till her mother rebelled! The plans, however, had already been made.

'All right,' she smiled, 'though they already have the plans. I'm thankful to resolve the question of the tapestries so easily. That is, if Miss Cook decides to come to us.'

'She'll come,' said Mrs. Wyatt. 'Don't worry about that. She'll come all right.'

She got up and made her way out of the room, and Anne turned to Helen. The other girl was also looking at the clock.

'Gracious, I must fly! Try to see Caroline soon, won't you, Anne?'

'I'll try,' promised Anne.

The words, in Helen's flute-like voice, seemed to hang in the air after Anne was left alone and memory stirred again.

Caroline . . . the only way to get Mother to accept Caroline . . .

The words again hung in the air, and the colour began to drain out of Anne's cheeks. She remembered overhearing them when she met Helen for the first time. Was it this girl whom Francis had wanted to marry? Had there been a row because Mrs. Wyatt refused to accept her?

Yet why, if that was the reason, hadn't

Francis just gone off and married her? After all, it was just what had happened with her. Had he been in love with Caroline and felt she wasn't 'right' for Elvan?

Anne paused, her thoughts probing, though she did not want to examine them too closely. Just why had Francis insisted on their hurried wedding before he went off to America? Perhaps the real reason was something to do with Caroline Cook.

4

Anne made time to walk over to Cravenhill the following day. As yet she felt very strange to the area around Elvan, but the beauty of her surroundings almost took her breath away. She paused on a bridge which spanned the river, looking down on a delightful picturesque old house built near a small but very beautiful church. The river divided nearby, forming an island which flamed with colour from masses of flowers, shrubs and trees.

Anne lingered, feeling suddenly at peace with the world as she strolled over to the other side of the bridge, staring down the valley where the river flowed swiftly and smoothly, the water clear, pure and unpolluted. Occasionally a salmon leapt for a fly, the displaced water forming concentric rings, ever more increasing, then decreasing again as the river surged onwards. A range of hills formed a backcloth which caught and held her gaze, shimmering in the warmth of the day, then with a small sigh Anne walked on, remembering to go straight ahead at the crossroads till she came to a farm gateway marked 'Cravenhill'.

The farm was very neat and tidy with well-kept buildings and a good solid farmhouse, fresh with cream paint and flower beds on either side of the front door. It was hard to imagine that Helen Wyatt had come here as a child, and gone home again 'smelling of the farmyard'. Anne found the farmyard smell of the present day pleasant and warm with welcome.

She rang the bell, and smiled when a plump woman in her thirties opened the door.

'Mrs. Cook?' asked Anne. 'I'm Anne Wyatt from Elvan Hall. I wondered if I might see Miss Caroline Cook, please.'

The smile had left the woman's face, and her gaze became faintly hostile as she studied Anne for a long moment before answering. Then she opened the door wider and stood aside.

'Please come in, Mrs. Wyatt. I shall have to find Caroline for you, I'm afraid. We're very busy at the moment, and she's been helping.'

'I shan't take up too much of her time,' promised Anne. 'I've called on business, though, so I hope Miss Cook will have time to spare to talk to me.'

The small room into which Anne was shown was very pleasant, and sparkled with cleanliness. Richly coloured rugs glowed against polished wood floors, and Anne chose to sit on an old wooden settle by the window, listening to the pleasant farmyard sounds which wafted through the open door.

Presently she heard Mrs. Cook returning, and Anne stood up as a very small dark girl walked into the room. She was tiny, thought Anne, looking down at Caroline Cook from her superior height, as Beatrice Cook introduced them. She was like a small sprite who had come in out of the woods with her large faun-like eyes, cloudy dark hair and piquant little face.

'How do you do, Mrs. Wyatt?' Caroline said, politely but rather warily, as she eyed Anne with obvious reserve. She excused her businesslike clothes of blue corduroy slacks and a white shirt blouse. 'I . . . I'm afraid we're rather busy today.'

'I hope I won't keep you a moment,' said Anne quickly. 'In fact, I could perhaps make another appointment to come back and see you, if today isn't convenient. I should have telephoned first of all . . . '

She could feel the girl's hostility as she stared at her, and wondered if she shouldn't make her excuses and go quickly.

'Not at all,' said Caroline. 'Er . . . ' She glanced at Beatrice, who made for the kitchen door.

'I'll make a cup of tea.'

'Thank you,' said Anne, with a smile.

'I should welcome some tea.'

A moment later both girls were left alone to weigh each other up.

'You are . . . Helen's friend?' asked Anne, rather warily, and Caroline nodded.

'We've known each other since we were children.'

Anne deliberated, wondering how to broach the subject. Now that she had seen Caroline, she found her heart doing strange things, almost as though she were viewing the girl's beauty with dismay. She couldn't imagine Francis knowing this lovely dark elf of a girl and not falling in love with her. Yet, if that were so, why hadn't he married Caroline? Why had he chosen her instead?

'I . . . er . . . I believe you do needlework.'

'I have a degree in embroidery.'

'And you're going to work in London?'

'Not till September. I'm going to Goldsmith's College in London to do a post-graduate course in embroidery.'

'I see. I . . . ah . . . wondered if you'd be interested in taking on a special job at Elvan Hall. We're at the moment renovating the old house.'

'I know.'

Caroline's voice was quiet, but Anne thought she detected a rather odd note, as though this had meant a great deal to her.

'There are a few lovely tapestries and chaircovers, etc., which require an expert hand on them to carry out repairs. I wondered if you could take it on,' said Anne simply.

'Did Helen send you?' asked Caroline quickly. 'Does Mrs. Wyatt know?'

'Helen did mention that you could do the job, but only after I said I would try to find someone. And Mrs. Wyatt does know . . . yes.'

Caroline bit her lip, the lovely pink flush on her cheeks enhancing her queer elfin beauty.

'Does . . . Francis know you've asked me?'

This time Anne paused, wondering if she ought to point out that all this was her business, not Caroline's. Then she remembered that this girl had known the Wyatts all her life.

'He knows I'm doing everything possible to make Elvan Hall a place of beauty again, and that I'm preserving all that is good and beautiful there. He knows I shall employ someone to do the embroidery, and would no doubt consider it very sensible that the someone should be you.'

Caroline's colour had come and gone, leaving her slightly pinched.

Again Anne began to wish she hadn't come, and that she was, perhaps, making a mistake. But surely the girl would not accept the job if there really had been anything between her and Francis.

'I could always get someone from London, I suppose,' she began, 'if you aren't interested . . . '

'I am,' said Caroline quickly.

'I would want to see samples of your work, and how much would you expect to be paid?'

'Oh, I should be happy to do it without . . . '

'That would be unthinkable. This is a professional job, and would require to be treated professionally.'

There was an awkward silence, while Caroline Cook sat down, looking rather withdrawn.

'Perhaps you'd like to think it over and I could come back and see you . . . say in two or three days' time?'

Caroline nodded slowly.

'I should be free to see you on Wednesday,' she said, 'and to come to . . . to the Hall, if that would help. It would save you coming all the way over here.'

'No. As I say, I should want to see samples of your work, and I presume you have them at home?'

'Yes . . . yes, I have quite a few. I can get them all ready for you.'

'That would be splendid.'

She looked up with a smile as Beatrice Cook tapped on the door and came in carrying a solid looking wooden tray.

'I hope I'm not interrupting?' she asked, hardly disguising her curiosity.

'No, we've talked enough for the moment,' Anne told her smoothly. 'I shall come again to see Miss Cook on Wednesday.'

'Surely she can save you the trouble . . . '

'It's all arranged, Beatrice,' Caroline told her. 'Mrs. Wyatt would like to see me again on Wednesday. She has offered me a job. I . . . I shall have to think it over.'

'A job?'

'Only temporary, I'm afraid,' said Anne.

The older woman looked slightly relieved.

'She has a job,' she said, rather flatly.

'Only temporary,' said Caroline again. 'At . . . at the Hall.'

Their eyes seemed to challenge each

other, and Anne felt that an understanding had passed between them. Beatrice quickly changed the subject and offered Anne a cup of rather strong dark tea.

It was refreshing, however, and Anne drank it gratefully, while she talked on general subjects, saying how much she admired the beauty of the surrounding countryside.

'Yes, it's very beautiful,' Beatrice Cook agreed. 'Have you got to know Cockermouth yet?'

'Not very well, but I find it a charming town and a worthy setting for the Wordsworth Memorial. There was certainly much to inspire the poet around here.'

There was rather a long awkward silence.

'I shall walk back home again,' Anne said, rising. It was strange and delightful to think of Elvan Hall as home. She looked at Caroline, seeing a dark look in the girl's eyes, as though she could read her mind.

'You didn't ride over?'

'No, I walked. It isn't far, surely.'

'It's almost a mile and a half.'

'So far?'

Anne was surprised. It had not seemed such a long way.

'Nevertheless I like to walk,' she said firmly. 'Good afternoon, Mrs. Cook . . . Miss Cook.'

'Good afternoon,' echoed Beatrice, while Caroline shook hands again.

'I'll come,' said Caroline suddenly. 'Back to the Hall, I mean. I'll . . . be glad to do the job . . . I've decided.'

'Oh.' Anne felt slightly taken aback. 'I still think you ought to think it over,' she said firmly, 'and I do want to see your work. Decide on a fair salary, too.'

'Very well,' Caroline agreed.

Anne could almost feel the other girl's eyes on her as she walked down the drive to the main road. Had she been wise in inviting this girl to the Hall? she wondered. There were things she didn't know, things which had obviously happened in the past which had left their mark on both families. Was she wise in making these arrangements without any knowledge of what had gone before? Francis had known that the tapestries needed to be repaired. Why hadn't he arranged for Caroline to do it, even if his mother had disagreed? And come to that, why *had* Mrs. Wyatt been so against having Caroline asked about the job? Guiltily Anne felt that the older woman's opposition had prompted her to ask the girl!

Anne's thoughts were rather more disturbed as she walked along the main road, even though darting birds, and the occasional drone of a bee made the warm fresh air relaxing and slightly soporific. Anne realised that she was tired, and decided to rest in her room before tea, but already Helen was on the look-out for her.

'Did you ask her?' she said eagerly. 'What did she say? Did she say she'd come?'

'I've asked her to think it over,' Anne

told her flatly. 'There's much still to be decided.'

'She'll come,' said Helen confidently. 'She loves Elvan. It should have belonged to Caroline.'

Anne's fatigue made her suddenly angry.

'What do you mean?' she asked, her eyes flashing a little. 'Why should this place belong to Caroline Cook?'

Helen's eyes dropped.

'She loves it so,' she repeated stubbornly. 'Caroline would make it beautiful.'

'That's surely our hope,' said Anne. 'That's why she's being asked to come.'

She left Helen and mounted the stairs, her head high. It wasn't Caroline's home, it was hers. Hers and Francis's. She had nothing at all to fear from Caroline Cook.

5

Once a week Anne wrote to Judith, as well as her own parents. With Francis it was different, as she gave him an account of all the happenings at Elvan, writing a short paragraph daily. She felt it was the best thing she could do for him, keeping him well up to date with home news.

She missed young Judith, however. Now and again she had caught a rather frightened look in the little girl's eyes, and felt that Judith was over-dominated by her mother, who was inclined to shout a repeated order to the child.

'She behaves as though she were stupid at times,' she complained to Anne.

'She's not at all stupid,' Anne had defended. 'She's very intelligent.'

Mrs. Wyatt had grunted, as though asking Anne what she knew about

103

Judith, and now she felt she knew the child very well indeed, and was looking forward to having her home during the summer holidays.

There seemed to be little social life, apart from one or two events for charity, which Anne attended, even though she knew her presence might be the subject for gossip. Helen had gone with her once or twice, and Anne had been glad of her, but she found that people were very kind, and were willing to accept her as Francis's new wife. Anne knew that she would have to play a bigger part in charitable affairs after she had settled in, but she thought she would enjoy this, and find it of interest.

A day or two after she had been to see Caroline Cook, the telephone rang and a smooth, rather rich voice asked to speak to Miss Wyatt. The line was rather indistinct and Anne paused.

'Miss or Mrs?' she asked, her brows wrinkling. No doubt it was another invitation to a function.

'Miss, of course,' the voice laughed

lazily in her ear. 'Is that you Helen darling, trying to pull my leg?'

'No, this is Mrs. Wyatt,' said Anne firmly. 'Miss Wyatt is round at the stables, if you'd care to hang on. Or would you prefer that she rang you back?'

There was silence, broken only by gentle breathing.

'It will take ages to bring her over . . . er . . . Mrs. Wyatt. No, I'll ring back in . . . say . . . thirty minutes?'

'Very well,' agreed Anne. 'Who shall I say is calling?'

But the line had gone dead, and Anne put down the telephone, considering. So Helen had a boyfriend? It was strange she had never mentioned a young man, though now and again she had gone out looking very smart and well-groomed. Anne speculated. She hadn't liked the sound of the rather fruity, confident voice.

However, it was Helen's business, not hers. The man was Helen's friend, and no doubt she knew him well enough to judge him. Anne looked at the time. It wasn't likely that Helen would be back within the next half hour, so she would just have to slip a jacket on over her silk dress, and go round to the stables to find her.

The stables were situated away from the house, across a cobbled yard, and after Anne had poked her head into the tack room and found it empty, she walked round a corner to find Helen putting a shoe on one of the horses, assisted by a tall, wellbuilt young man. Anne had met David Mellor before and liked him a lot.

Peter Birkett, the young veterinary surgeon, also stood nearby, and he turned to smile at Anne as she approached. He was thin beside David, but he looked strong and wiry, the wind ruffling his dark curly hair.

Helen looked well in her own environment, and Anne stood watching her for a moment, admiring the girl's deft skill with the horse.

'Well, this is an honour,' she said,

106

straightening up. 'It isn't often we see you here.'

'It isn't often I'm invited,' said Anne equably.

This time Helen flushed.

'Oh . . . well, I didn't think you cared about horses.'

'Well, I do. Who's this chap here?'

'Elvan Prince,' said Helen, her eyes shining a little. 'He's going to make our name one day, aren't you, my precious?'

Helen's hand went up to stroke the soft dark neck, which shone with grooming. Both young men watched her indulgently.

'He was fourth last time we raced him.'

'Are they all for racing . . . all the horses, I mean?'

'Gracious, no. The others are for hunting.'

'Foxes?'

'Yes.'

Anne frowned.

'I hate the thought of an animal

being hunted to its death.'

'But not the thought of the animals hunted by the fox?'

'It's a wild creature. It doesn't know any better.'

Helen's eyes were gleaming.

'Don't make quick judgements, Anne. It's the only way to keep the foxes down on those fells, and while he's young and healthy, he'll get away. He's a wily chap, is our fox, you know. He's by no means a defenceless animal, and if you saw the damage he does, you might not be so sympathetic.'

Anne said nothing. Perhaps Helen's was good advice. She would get to know more about it before voicing dogmatic opinions. Nevertheless, she still hated hunting.

'If you're going to argue over hunting,' Peter Birkett put in, smiling, 'I'm off! See you later, Helen. Goodbye, Mrs. Wyatt.'

'Drop in tomorrow if you can, Peter,' Helen called after him.

Anne watched him go, then turned again to Helen.

'Where are the ponies?' she asked.

Again Helen's eyes softened.

'Up there in that field, but you can see our Peter Pan over here in the field behind the stables.' They wandered over the cobbles together, and Helen called loudly for the small Shetland pony, a truly beautiful chestnut with a flaxen mane and tail. Anne knew that Peter had won many prizes, including Breed Champion at the last show, and she delighted in the small sturdy pony who plodded over to the fence to nuzzle Helen's fingers.

'He's lovely,' she said sincerely.

'Yes, he is,' Helen agreed.

'And you keep the ponies for breeding?'

Helen nodded. 'Children love Shetland ponies, and occasionally they're even bought to be harnessed to a small trap. They make lovely pets, though.'

Anne's eyes were alight with interest, and she thought how charming Helen looked without the carefully withdrawn look on her face when they were having a normal discussion. They could be friends, thought Anne, if only Helen would come to accept her as Francis' wife.

Suddenly she remembered why she had come, and glanced quickly at her watch.

'Heavens! I forgot.'

'What?'

'You're wanted on the phone. A man rang up half an hour ago and said he would ring back. We'd better hurry if you want to speak to him, though he didn't give his name.'

Helen had flushed scarlet.

'Why didn't you tell me at once?' she asked crossly. 'I might miss him!'

'Surely he'll keep trying till he gets you . . . on the phone, I mean,' cried Anne, running after her.

But already Helen was racing to the house. Anne gave up, and walked after her slowly. She was going through the hall when she heard

Helen's voice on the phone.

'Of course, Roger, I'd love to . . . of course not . . . yes, I can be ready for seven . . .'

Anne mounted the stairs slowly, to wash and change before tea. Normally she would have been pleased to hear Helen speaking so warmly to a young man on the telephone, but something was making her uneasy. There was something rather young and trusting about Francis' sister, in spite of her upbringing, and Anne hadn't liked the sound of that smooth voice at the other end of the telephone. Voices, she thought, were a bit like handshakes. You reacted instinctively.

Suddenly she wished that Francis would be home again soon, though there was no date yet fixed for his return.

And tomorrow she was going to prepare the drawing room for the decorators to start, and Mrs. Wyatt was insisting that she saw the men before they started the job. Anne couldn't guess why this was so important, as the colours had already been chosen for the plans, and she had no intention of making any changes.

She met Helen again on the stairs.

'I shall be going out tonight, Anne,' she said, her eyes twinkling almost with mischief. 'I shan't be in for dinner.'

'I hope you have a lovely evening,' Anne told her sincerely, and Helen smiled.

'I shall.'

'Can I help in any way?' asked Anne impulsively. 'I mean, I can let you have some of the perfume Francis gave me.'

'To get the smell of the stable away? I *do* bath, you know, Anne.'

The colour surged to her cheeks. Why should Helen misinterpret a generous gesture? She had only wanted to . . . perhaps to share a little in the evening, and surely Helen should know she had not been making tactless remarks, since the other girl was always as fresh as a daisy after her days in the open air.

'Don't be silly,' she said sharply. 'You *know* I don't mean that.'

'Oh, all right. I'm sorry. Only leave me alone to choose things for myself.'

Anne watched her go, then slowly she went on downstairs. Suddenly Elvan Hall seemed very lonely indeed.

★ ★ ★

At dinner Anne shared a rather silent meal with Mrs. Wyatt. The older woman obviously had something on her mind, judging by the frown on her forehead, and finally she cleared her throat.

'Who is this man who's taking Helen out?' she asked at length.

'I don't know,' Anne told her. 'He rang up, but he didn't give his name. I . . . I rather thought you would know.'

'Hmph!'

'It's good for her to have time off and enjoy herself,' Anne defended, 'though I wish . . . ' She broke off. She could hardly comment about her

113

uneasiness to Mrs. Wyatt, especially since she had nothing, really, to go on.

'You wish what?'

'That he'd called for Helen. He sounded . . . plausible, sort of smooth . . . I don't know.'

'Unsuitable, you mean?'

There was a look on Mrs. Wyatt's face which made Anne's cheeks colour.

'I tell you, I don't know,' she said again, rather sharply.

'One's children do extremely ill-considered things these days,' Mrs. Wyatt said heavily, and there was no mistaking her meaning. Anne looked consideringly at her mother-in-law. For better or worse they were stuck with one another, and on impulse she leaned forward.

'Why can't we pull together?' she asked. 'Francis belongs to both of us in a way. It would be easier if we pulled our weight together.'

'I agree,' the other woman said deliberately, 'only you seem to be

114

bent on holding all the reins yourself.'

'I'm only shouldering my own responsibilities.'

'And making a fool of yourself at times, girl!'

Anne flushed again. Their meal that evening had been less appetising than usual, because she had recommended alternative cuts of meat.

'All right, so I make mistakes. Can't you help me to learn?'

'Why should I? If Francis had listened to me, he'd have found a girl who doesn't have to be taught. I told him so before.'

'Before what?'

Mrs. Wyatt heaved herself out of her chair.

'It doesn't matter now. I'm going upstairs. I feel rather tired.'

'I'm sorry,' said Anne. 'Goodnight.'

'G'night,' muttered Mrs. Wyatt, and Anne sighed a little, though at least she had received an answer.

★ ★ ★

The day before the decorators were due to start on the drawing room, Anne spent the morning tidying drawers and cupboards. She had been to see Caroline Cook the previous afternoon, and felt very satisfied that the girl's work was excellent. Caroline was starting work on Monday, and was going to give Anne her opinion on how much work was needed to renovate the old tapestries. She had also found some delicately worked bed-covers, and some old samplers which might look very nice if they were framed.

Helen was delighted that Caroline was taking on the work, and threw rather malicious glances at her mother, who clearly didn't care for Caroline. She and Helen had been having words over the girl's friendship with Roger Baxter, the man who had telephoned her.

'Who is he?' demanded Mrs. Wyatt.

'A friend of mine.'

'Don't be impertinent!'

'But he *is* a friend. I met him in

Carlisle and Teresa Elliott introduced us. He's a company director.'

'What sort of company?'

'I don't know. Honestly, Mummy, do lay off. I can decide for myself who my friends are, thank you very much.'

'First Francis, now you,' said Mrs. Wyatt sourly, and this time Anne's lips tightened.

She was still thinking about Mrs. Wyatt as she tidied up bundles of old bills and clipped them neatly with bulldog clips.

There was an old sheet of paper with closely written notes, difficult to read, which fascinated her, and she sat down to read notes on otter hunting which had taken place almost a hundred years ago, a diary kept most probably by a member of the family or some friend of an earlier Wyatt. She read that in the first half of the nineteenth century, otter-hounds were kept in small numbers in different parts of the county, and used for hunting otters and foulmarts, or polecats. A full-strength pack numbered ten couple and this particular pack included a Newfound-land dog.

Anne read on, fascinated yet repelled, that in December of 1837 an otter was dragged from Bassenthwaite Beck into the side of Dash waterfall and over a hilltop adjoining Skiddaw, then down the watershed of the River Ellen, where it was killed.

She shivered a little at the mental picture this invoked, and put the papers back again, going to the window to look out at her favourite view, which was of a long sweep of garden, bright with herbaceous borders, protected by tall, stately silver birch trees, pines, firs and cedars, and the bright sparkling river beyond, where otters had been hunted to their death.

Yet she herself had been furious with the owls when she saw the wreck of a wren's nest.

Anne finished tidying the room and tried to imagine it with fresh ivory walls instead of the present neglected-looking buff colour. The lovely old panelling could be polished until it reflected the light, and the carpet and curtains were still good. The chairs and tapestries would look splendid after Caroline Cook had worked on them.

Anne felt a sudden surge of happiness and satisfaction, and a strange inner excitement at the thought of seeing Francis again. She was sure he would be pleased with everything she had done, and she thought how nice it would be if it had all been finished before his return. However, in his last letter he said that his business transactions might be concluded fairly quickly, as problems were gradually being ironed out.

★ ★ ★

'You're a fool,' said Mrs. Wyatt to Anne, having called her up to her bedroom on Monday morning.

Anne said nothing. She was well aware that Mrs. Wyatt thought her a fool.

'You've brought that girl here after all.'

'She's doing a splendid job of work,' defended Anne. 'There's so much beauty in this house, so much fine work which is going to be spoiled through neglect. I don't intend that to happen. Caroline has been trained to save that sort of thing, so it seems to me very sensible to employ her to do it.'

'She's after Francis. I don't know why I should bother telling you that, but I don't want more scandal in the house. The Wyatts haven't always been discreet. And Helen will only encourage her. She wanted her to have Francis in the first place, but I put my foot down. I stopped her games, and for once, Francis seemed to listen to me, which I may as well tell you was a surprise. He's far too fond of going his own way. But you go inviting her back here again. You're a fool, Anne Wyatt!'

Anne caught her breath. So there had been something after all. Yet why had Mrs. Wyatt waited till she had Caroline actually working in the house before telling her all this? Why hadn't she told her so when she knew she had gone to see the girl in the first place?

'Why haven't you told me this before?' she asked, anger and a spark of fear making her voice husky.

'Why should I? I thought you learned by mistakes and wouldn't be such a fool. Besides, I gave you a broad enough hint.'

'Foolishness and ignorance aren't the same, are they? I'd no knowledge of what happened . . . ' She bit her lip. 'Did . . . did Francis want to marry her?' she asked in a small voice, and for a moment there was a slight softening in the darting gaze of the older woman.

'He's a man, isn't he?' she demanded, 'and she's a soft, pretty little thing. She's full of feminine wiles, making herself look pretty and helpless, then showing how clever she is with her

121

needle. A very womanly pursuit. She clings, too, so don't think you'll get rid of her easily. Get her in, and you can't get her back out!'

Anne stared back.

'I've no intention of getting her back out till the job is finished,' she said, with a lift of her chin. 'I've employed her, and I hope to see that she carries out the work which needs to be done. After that, I've no doubt she will be going to London to take up her post-graduate course.'

'You hope!'

'I've no reason to think otherwise,' said Anne quietly.

'You must be very sure that Francis is deeply in love with you.'

The eyes which looked at her were veiled, and Anne felt the hot colour rush to her cheeks, and fear swept over her like a sickness. Francis didn't love her. In fact, she suspected now that Francis might still be in love with Caroline, but in some way this rather selfish woman had spoiled things for him. What could she have said, which made Francis heed her for once?

The colour began to drain from Anne's cheeks leaving her pale and tired-looking.

'Francis can surely arrange his own life, can't he?' she asked quietly. 'He's a grown man, and my husband.'

She stopped, desperately wanting to know more, to probe the past and to have more idea as to how Francis had felt about Caroline, and what strong weapon had been used to break it up. But she knew it was no good asking questions, and pride kept her tongue stilled in any case.

'I'm getting up now,' Mrs. Wyatt said, rather peevishly. 'I want to see those decorators anyway, to see if they're brightening up that appalling drawing room. It's like the Black Hole of Calcutta.'

'It will look beautiful when the walls have been painted ivory,' Anne told her. 'It's just the dark ceiling which makes it look so dull.'

'I've always said it's too dark, but Henry wouldn't have it any other way. Francis is almost as bad. I hate all this gloom.'

This time Anne smiled. That was evident in the bright frills of Mrs. Wyatt's bedroom. She loved soft fluffy things.

'Tell Mrs. Hansett I want her,' she called as Anne turned towards the door.

'Very well.'

'And throw that girl out, if you've any sense.'

Could it be that for once, Mrs. Wyatt was on her side? wondered Anne wryly.

★　★　★

It was after lunch before Anne had time to look in at the drawing room and see what impression, if any so far, that the painters were making. Caroline had elected to go home for lunch, and Anne breathed a small sigh of relief. She hadn't relished a meal with Mrs. Wyatt either scowling

124

or being openly rude to the girl.

The information that Mrs. Wyatt had given her about Caroline had tended to make her view the girl rather differently, making her seem even lovelier with her dainty slenderness. It was easy to imagine Francis in love with her, thought Anne with a sudden fierce pang of jealousy, as she looked at the soft cloud of dark hair falling over Caroline's face, as she bent over her stitching. Anne had provided her with all she needed, in a corner of the morning room, and Caroline had laid out her materials on a spacious table where she could work comfortably.

Mrs. Wyatt grumbled that there was nowhere decent left to sit in, and went off in the huff to her room. This was untrue, as Elvan Hall was plentifully provided with public rooms, and the central heating could easily be switched on if she wished. Anne had made herself unpopular by switching it off until evening during the warmer days.

'You'll freeze us all to death,' Mrs.

Wyatt had declared, pulling on a woollen jacket.

'On days like these?' asked Anne. 'That's nonsense! You could even sit outside on the summer seat, and feel the warmth of the sun on your face.'

'And get eaten alive by insects. Besides, there's a draught. If you won't switch on the heating, I'll have my fire.'

So Mrs. Wyatt's bedroom became a hothouse of warm air, while the others were glad of a cooling breeze, now and again, coming up from the river.

The painters, an elderly man and young boy, sang and whistled merrily as they pulled out furniture and moved planks. Helen looked pink-cheeked and excited — almost too excited, thought Anne uneasily, and took every opportunity of talking to Caroline and inviting her out to the stables to look at the horses.

'But I'm here to work,' the girl protested, glancing at Anne.

'Surely she can just come over to the stables for five minutes!' protested

126

Helen, and Anne nodded.

'I'm sure Caroline will plan her time here properly,' she agreed, and watched the girls run along, side by side. She'd had her own girl friends at school, but most of them were married now, with families. But it would be nice to have a friend, she thought rather wistfully. It was easy to see now that Helen would much prefer to have had Caroline here all the time.

Anne wandered along the corridor, promising Mrs. Hansett that she would come along and help her with one or two things very shortly.

'I'll just look in at the drawing room,' she said, making for the heavy oak door.

'Very well, ma'am,' the housekeeper smiled.

Mrs. Hansett approved of Anne. The kitchen staff might have to mind things a little more, but Mrs. Hansett preferred it that way. Things were no longer so lackadaisical, she thought, as she made her way to the kitchen.

Anne was bereft of words as she stood in the large drawing room, where everything was covered with large sheets, and the young boy painter had started to put a first coat of paint on the dark wood panelling. Anne was so appalled that she couldn't find a word to say for the first minute.

'Stop!' she gasped. 'For heaven's sake, stop! Whoever gave you permission to paint that panelling?'

The boy turned to stare at her, then the older man slowly descended the ladder.

'I thought it was funny,' he confessed, 'but the lady of the house said to paint it all white, that it needed brightening up, and that the plans had been changed.'

'I'm the lady of the house,' said Anne, her eyes flashing.

'The older lady . . . Mrs. Wyatt,' protested the painter. 'She told us. She really did say the plans were changed.'

'They were not changed. I thought I

made that clear to you.'

The man looked uncomfortable.

'Oh aye, miss . . . ma'am . . . only it wasn't clear who had the right of it, you see. You or her.'

'You could have asked!'

'Asked who? Her or you?'

Anne bit her lip.

'I'm afraid it will have to be cleaned off,' she said firmly.

'Cleaned off! But . . . but that's well-nigh impossible, miss. It's . . . '

'I don't care how impossible it is, it will have to be cleaned off,' said Anne firmly. 'You do not paint carved oak panelling, centuries old, and polished with age.'

The man pushed a hand through his hair.

'No, I wouldn't have thought so, but . . . well, it will take time. It'll be costly, too. Thank God there's only a little bit done.'

This time Anne gave no thought to be economical.

'I don't care *what* it costs,' she said,

her eyes flashing. 'It must be cleaned off.'

She looked at it again, her panic rising. Whatever would Francis say? Now she was beginning to understand his insistence that she took charge of the work which had to be carried out. Only she hadn't . . . she'd let him down. She should have checked up on it all along the way, but her head had been so full of fears over Francis and Caroline, and her own efforts at deciding whether to allow the girl to keep coming, or if it would be wiser to send her home. Yet the renovations had to be considered, and Anne had put that first. Now she was furious with herself for not checking on the painters, too.

Anne hurried from the room, a cold sickness in her heart, and mounted the stairs to her mother-in-law's bedroom. This time they really were going to have it out!

★ ★ ★

'The place has been like a mausoleum for years,' protested Mrs. Wyatt. 'Henry promised me I could brighten it up, then he wouldn't allow it to be touched. No woman has been allowed to bring a bit of taste to the place for generations.'

'I'd hardly call painting beautiful carved oak panelling bringing taste to the place,' said Anne hotly. 'Francis trusted me to look after it, and now you . . . you went behind my back!'

'If I hadn't it would still be the same dull room,' Mrs. Wyatt told her balefully. 'I could make this house a place of beauty, fresh and bright with a . . . a sort of lightness to the place. But I was never given my head, and now . . . now Francis has handed it over to you and you're obviously going to toe the line, like all the rest. I think I might at least have had my chance.'

Anne sat at the foot of the bed. For some reason she began to feel sympathy for the older woman who would probably have been much happier in a different sort of home from the Hall.

'The panelling has only improved with age,' she said gently. 'It's beautiful. It was made with love, and generations of women have looked after it with love, and its beauty was enhanced by its patina. When you paint it, that's all swept away by each stroke of the brush. Don't you see? . . . anyone coming after who prefers the original panelling would find it almost impossible to remove the paint, and keep what was already there. As it is, heaven knows what harm has been done . . . '

Her voice trailed off forlornly, but Mrs. Wyatt was more angry than sorry.

'It's ridiculous to waste time and money going back,' she said, her eyes sparkling. 'The only way is to take one's courage in both hands and order the job to be done. It takes one woman with an individual mind to be firm. No doubt everyone will enjoy the freshness and brightness and will bless me when it becomes a *fait accompli*. I don't see how you can order the men to remove what's been done, Anne. You'd be much better to accept it, and enjoy it, as we're all likely to do.'

Anne stared at her for a long time, then rose slowly to her feet. It was no use talking. Her father-in-law must have been a strong man to have kept Mrs. Wyatt in check for so many years!

'I'm feeling unwell again,' Mrs. Wyatt said peevishly. 'That girl upsets me, and Helen is going out again with that strange man. If he's a proper person for her to associate with, then he should be calling here for her, not ringing her up and asking her to meet him in Carlisle.'

This time Anne was in complete agreement with her mother-in-law.

'Surely Helen has sense enough to judge people she meets, and to recognise if they're worthwhile or not,' she said slowly. 'I mean, a girl of her age . . .'

'In other words, I should have brought her up better able to choose her friends,' said Mrs. Wyatt dryly, and Anne flushed again. The thought *had* crossed her mind.

'We can only be taught to recognise good value, then left to find it ourselves,' she said defensively.

'And you found it?'

'Yes.'

Anne's tone was emphatic, and there was an unreadable gleam in the older woman's eyes.

'Then you've nothing to worry about, have you?' she asked blandly, and Anne hesitated, feeling slightly at a loss. Her efforts at having it out with her mother in-law seemed to have accomplished nothing. They were just different kinds of people and Anne visualised the years ahead when she would have to keep fighting for what she considered to be right for Elvan Hall.

Her hand caressed the beautiful wood on the banister rail as she descended the stairs, the smell of paint and turpentine from the drawing room making her heartsick with frustration and disappointment. Would the men succeed in undoing the damage before Francis got home? She had been so looking forward to the room being completely finished, and she had visualised just how she would arrange it by altering the position of several small items, and placing bowls of flowers, which she had learned to arrange while she still lived at the Manse.

But now she felt worried in case the panelling would never look the same again. Luckily very little had been painted so far, and could, perhaps, be hidden with an item of furniture. Nevertheless there was no disguising the fact that the patina was going to be spoiled.

6

Anne felt a headache coming on as she made for the small morning room, where Caroline would no doubt be packing up, ready to go home. She would just check up on the work she had already done.

But as Anne rounded the corridor at the foot of the stairs, she heard the sound of voices, and a moment later she was looking along the corridor to where Francis stood, the morning-room door open, as well as the drawing-room door opposite.

Anne's heart turned to ice at the expression on his face, and she could hear Caroline's light voice greeting him half-fearfully, then Francis closed the door with a sharp click and strode towards her down the corridor, his dark eyes flashing in his white face, his mouth grim with compressed lips.

'Francis?' she said nervously, then felt a lump catching her throat. 'Oh, Francis! I'm so glad to see you.'

For a moment he wavered, catching her to him and kissing her. Then the fury was back in him.

'I've no doubt, and I shall be very glad of a word with you, Anne. In here.'

He propelled her into the study, and shut the door, before turning her to face him, his fingers biting into her arm.

'Can you please explain why some of our lovely old wood panelling is being painted, and why you thought fit to invite Caroline Cook to this house?'

'I . . . I didn't expect you home so soon,' she stammered.

'Obviously.'

'I . . . I . . . it was a mistake . . . about the panelling, I mean.'

'I'm glad to hear it!'

She bit her lip at the granite-like expression on his face. How could she talk to him when he was so hard in his anger that his ears were closed to reasons and explanations? Besides, how could she blame it on Mrs. Wyatt, when she had been left in charge?

'Obviously whatever I say won't make any difference, Francis,' she said quietly. 'You aren't in the mood to listen to reason.'

'Beautiful panelling spoilt and you expect me to listen to reason! I left you here in charge as my wife. I thought I could trust you to carry out my wishes because they were *your* wishes, too, but instead . . . instead . . .'

He choked on his anger, and she felt waves of sickness pass over her as she tried to keep her wits about her. She couldn't blame him for his rage. Her own feelings had been almost as intense, though her natural desire to seek for explanations had made her understand, and had tempered her own anger and disappointment. Francis had nothing with which to lessen his.

'I can only say I stopped the work immediately I found out, and the men are going to clean off what has already been done.'

'They will not lay a finger on it!' shouted Francis. 'They could cause as much ruin undoing their charming handiwork as they've caused in the first place. No, I shall have someone who knows something about it here as soon as possible. It will probably cost me a fortune!'

Her legs were trembling, and he pushed forward a chair, saying rather more gently: 'Sit down, Anne. And Caroline Cook? Why is she here?'

'To mend the tapestries and chair-covers, of course. All the old embroidered items such as pictures, panels, bedspreads. Didn't you know she had qualified in embroidery at university, and she's about to do a post-graduate course?'

He nodded. 'Of course I knew. If I'd wanted Caroline to do work, I'd have asked her myself.'

'Then why didn't you?' she asked, slow anger beginning to burn. He had been away for several weeks, but instead of being pleased to see her, he was giving her nothing but censure. Maybe she hadn't got his love, but she was his wife and surely entitled to some sort of affection. Instead, all he could do was criticise, without even trying to find out how far responsible she was for these mistakes.

'Why . . . ?'

'Didn't you? You must have known this work had to be done. It seems eminently sensible to me to ask this girl to do this work, when she lives nearby and is a friend of Helen's. I've seen samples of her work, and she's well qualified to do it. Surely it's perfectly natural for me to ask her, and I'm at a loss to understand your anger.'

'You know nothing about it,' he told her, his eyes flashing.

'Obviously. Do you want to tell me or shall I guess? Can it be that you're in love with her? Can it be that you regret not having her here permanently, instead of me?'

She stood up and faced him, her chin high and her eyes flashing as angrily as his own. For a long moment their eyes met, and she saw him struggling with some sort of strong emotion as he gripped her hands, then pulled her into his arms and kissed her fiercely, almost bruising her in his arms.

'There! Is that how I should welcome you?' he asked. 'Is that better?'

Again Anne felt a wave of sickness pass over her as she fought against the threatening tears.

'No, Francis,' she said quietly. 'No, that isn't the welcome I expected. I shall instruct Mrs. Hansett to prepare something for you if you need a meal, then . . . then I shall unpack for you. I'll see that Caroline leaves in the morning.'

'Oh, don't trouble,' he told her wearily. 'It doesn't matter now, anyway. She can stay and finish the job. You undertook to engage her, so we'll both honour that contract. As for a meal, I need none. I have work to do here at the desk.'

'Very well. I'll leave you to get on with it. Perhaps we can discuss things further tomorrow?'

He drew a hand across his forehead.

'There's nothing to discuss. I shall have the panelling put right. I shall also hire another firm of decorators who don't employ charlatans. I . . . ' he looked at her . . . 'I can no doubt guess as to how it happened, and I look to you to see that nothing further goes wrong. No doubt you'll be rather more vigilant from now on, but I expect you to oversee the rest of the work. *You* are the mistress here, not . . . not . . . ' His voice trailed off. 'My mother,' he muttered.

Anne left, a heavy dullness in her eyes. She was mistress here, but she wasn't his wife. She was being asked to love an empty shell. Slowly she climbed the stairs and went into the large bedroom they shared, then on impulse she removed her immediate necessities to the small room she used as a dressing room next door. It had a small bed in it, which, she understood, had been put there for the use of a nurse when Henry Wyatt had been so ill. It was quite big enough for her, and she sat down on it, her heart bruised and aching. She loved Francis, but she refused to share his bed while he regarded her as part of the fitments.

Perhaps he had cared for her a little, but anger and disappointment at her incompetence had soon dispelled that. He didn't really need a wife, she told herself bitterly. He only needed someone in whom he had vested the authority to run his home.

She was already in bed, but far from being asleep, when he came up that night. She heard him pause as he entered their bedroom, then cross the room quickly to open the door of the dressing room. She lay still, her heart pounding loud enough for him to hear, then after what seemed a lifetime, while he looked on her still form, he walked back out and closed the door with a sharp click.

It was then that the tears came, and Anne allowed them to soak her pillow, feeling that she would weep her heart out. What would tomorrow bring? she wondered. And a lifetime of tomorrows? How could she bear this house which offered her everything, except love?

* * *

Next day Francis had recovered a little from his initial rage and greeted Anne quietly, a rather carefully searching look in his eyes as he looked at her. A glance in the mirror that morning had told her that she wasn't at her best, and that her storm of weeping had given her shadowed eyes in a pale face.

'I trust you . . . slept well?' Francis said rather heavily, and her chin lifted.

'Thank you, I slept comfortably,' she returned evenly.

Helen joined them for breakfast, her

eyes speculative as she sensed the withdrawn atmosphere between them.

'The drawing room is rather a mess,' she said mischievously.

'It surprises me that you didn't anticipate something of the kind, Helen,' said Francis bitingly. 'You must have known Mother had this in mind.'

'You didn't leave *me* in charge,' said Helen pointedly, 'and anyway, I've enough to do with Goldie. She's caught a cold. Peter and I have been worried stiff about her.'

But not enough to keep her from going out with Roger Baxter, thought Anne, then felt ashamed of herself. David Mellor, the young groom, was no doubt thoroughly reliable and competent, and Helen could leave her precious horses in his charge with a completely free mind. Peter Birkett, the young vet, was also very responsible, and wouldn't let the horse be neglected.

'Caroline will be here soon,' said Helen, glancing at the clock, then at Francis from under lowered lids. 'She's making a marvellous job of all our old tapestries. She at least has a reverence for old treasures, and does her best to restore them.'

There was no mistaking her meaning and Anne felt a rush of anger against Helen. It was as though she were pointing out clearly to Francis that Caroline Cook would have been a better choice to leave in charge of Elvan Hall than she had been.

A moment later the door of the small room opened, and Caroline poked her head in. Anne felt surprised as Caroline had never before interrupted breakfast if they were a little late.

'Oh . . . oh, sorry,' she said, confused, and began to withdrawn uncertainly.

'No, come in, Caroline,' called Helen. 'Like a cup of coffee?'

'I . . . I was just about to start work,' the girl began, then immediately accepted the coffee, sitting down in a vacant chair.

This morning she looked as perfectly lovely as a miniature, her face delicately made up and her lovely hair brushed until it shone like silk. Anne was even more conscious of her own rather plain appearance. She glanced at Francis and saw that he was looking at Caroline and that the tight look was back on his mouth, as though he had to make a conscious effort to control his feelings for her.

'I love doing the tapestries, Francis,' she was saying softly. 'They're so beautiful, so well worth saving.'

'Yes,' he agreed stiffly.

She flushed and lowered her eyelids, and Anne again felt the sickness of jealousy.

'She does love him,' she thought miserably, 'and how could he help loving someone so pretty? She's like a piece of Dresden china.'

'I used to think how interesting they were when you used to show them to me,' Caroline went on bravely, because his face had darkened. 'In fact, I'm sure it's because of seeing all that lovely work that I took up embroidery in the first place. The designs are so marvellous. I've used part of the design in one of your old Persian rugs for a panel I did at Christmas. Would you like to see it some time?'

The small vivid face was eager, and Anne couldn't help her own interest.

'I'd love to see that,' she assured Caroline, then turned uncertainly to Francis.

'I'll bring it tomorrow,' the girl was saying. 'If . . . if that's all right.'

'That's perfectly all right,' he said stiffly. 'My wife will be most interested to see it, I'm sure.'

Anne heard the faint emphasis on the word 'wife' and her eyes flew to Caroline, seeing the colour leave the girl's face. As their eyes met, she could see how much the other girl had been hurt, and how much she still loved Francis. She felt an outsider suddenly, as though she were standing outside a circle which had been shattered and the pieces repaired haphazardly.

Francis was standing up, throwing his

napkin down carelessly on the table.

'I have to leave for Carlisle as soon as possible,' he told Anne, 'but first of all I want to speak to my mother. I'll go up to her room now. I . . . ' he hesitated as he strode towards the door, 'I'd like to see you, too, Anne, before I leave.'

'Very well, Francis,' she said quietly.

Caroline, too, was on her feet and excusing herself in order to start work in the morning room.

'What have you done to Francis, Anne darling?' asked Helen, the mischief back in her eyes, as she drank the last of her coffee.

'What do you mean?' she defended.

'He's even more of a bear than ever, yet once he . . . '

'Once he what?'

'Was such a darling,' said Helen, with a sigh. 'He was so sweet-tempered, and he wouldn't have dreamed of crossing Mummy. Though, of course, Daddy was here to make himself responsible for the place. And he and Caroline were so sweet together, a real boy and girl affair, though he was quite a bit older. He used to look after her as though she were a precious ornament of some kind, or one of his delicate wild creatures which needed protection. But now he's so unpredictable, as though he's been hurt, and is bent on taking it out of us all.'

'He has heavy responsibilities,' said Anne stiffly. 'He holds down a difficult job.'

'You should know, darling, since you were some sort of typist to him.'

'I was his secretary.'

'Of course.'

Helen buttoned up her jacket.

'Are you and he terribly in love, Anne?' she asked casually. 'I thought I knew about love, but you two!'

'What do you mean?' asked Anne, scarlet-cheeked.

'You could be married for years and years, you're so casual with one another. Now Roger and I . . . '

'It's serious, then?' asked Anne quickly. 'You and Mr. Baxter, I mean?'

'Don't change the subject. We're talking about you and Francis.'

'I don't want to discuss my relationship with Francis.'

'Nor I mine with Roger,' said Helen softly, her eyes dancing.

'But if you're serious, then why don't you bring him home?' asked Anne quickly. 'I'm sure Francis and . . . and your mother will want to meet him.'

'Francis didn't bring you home,' said Helen equably. 'Yet I'm sure Mother and I would like to have met you too . . . before you were married.'

'You were invited to the wedding,' said Anne.

'To see Francis marrying a stranger? Would you have gone in our place?'

Anne slowly shook her head. But the wedding hadn't been of her arranging. It had been Francis who wanted it that way.

'Was he making sure of you . . . or of himself?' asked Helen. 'I could understand a hurried engagement, but not a hurried wedding . . . not with Francis.'

No doubt from Helen's point of view, the hurried engagement would have been designed to show how much less suitable she was than Caroline. It would have been to win Mrs. Wyatt's approval . . . for Caroline!

But Francis had decided on marriage. Had that been ill-considered? Was he, even now, regretting it now that he had seen Caroline here in his own home again?

Anne was left alone to think about it, as Helen left the dining table. A moment later Mrs. Hansett appeared, and Anne helped her to clear the table on to the trolley. Upstairs the bedroom door had not been closed properly and Anne could hear the swift even tones of Francis' voice, interspersed with shrill comments from his mother.

A moment later they heard the bedroom door slam and Francis' quick footsteps on the stairs.

'I'll see to these, ma'am,' said the housekeeper, as she began to wheel away the trolley. 'I think Mr. Francis wants a word with you.'

Anne nodded, and walked towards the study where Francis appeared a moment later.

'I have someone coming to do the panel in two days' time,' he told her briskly. 'He's an expert on restoring old wood carvings. He may have to do the job over several days.'

'Oh, good,' said Anne, with relief. 'That's splendid.'

Francis rubbed a hand wearily over his face, and Anne had a sudden almost irresistible desire to run to him and put her arms round his neck to comfort him. But the thought of a rebuff kept her sitting still, well away from him, listening politely.

'I . . . I'm sorry it happened, Francis.'

'It can't be helped,' he said briefly. 'I . . . I shouldn't have blamed you. I realise I expected too much of you.'

She felt a stab of hurt, aware of his disappointment in her, and the hurt made the distance between them greater than ever.

Francis was regarding her searchingly, and thoughtfully.

'You're not happy,' he said abruptly.

'I . . . I . . . '

'No, I can see that you aren't happy. I . . . I made a mistake. I thought all this . . . ' he waved his hand around, ' . . . all this would make up for love, but I was wrong, wasn't I, Anne?'

No material thing ever made up for the absence of love, thought Anne forlornly, as she nodded.

Francis held his head in his hands, and again she longed to comfort him, but now it was impossible. He was recognising his own mistake in marrying her instead of Caroline, and Anne felt too wretched even to feel pain.

'I'm sorry, Anne,' he said quietly, 'but I'm asking you to try to make a go of it with me. We can't turn back, my dear. We've tied the knot too firmly to go back.'

Anne's cheeks flamed, knowing he was referring to the start of their marriage. There could be no question of having the marriage annulled, and divorce was also out of the question.

'Can we try to do a good job together?' Francis appealed, and she nodded wearily. He was right, there was no turning back. She was still her father's daughter, and she must stand by her vows.

He came round to stand behind her, then bent to kiss her check.

'Please,' she cried, 'I don't want . . . kindness.'

'Then what do you want?'

Some sort of positive emotion, she thought, her eyes darkly unhappy.

'It doesn't matter. Anything. I'm sorry, Francis, I didn't mean to be difficult. I . . . I suppose I just want common sense.'

He said nothing more, but picked up his briefcase and left.

Anne sat still for another few minutes, then went to find Mrs. Hansett. She still had a job to do. She was still mistress of Elvan Hall.

7

It seemed a long strange day to Anne, a day in which she tried hard to face up to the realities of her life. Mrs. Wyatt came downstairs looking peevish and short-tempered, but Anne didn't feel in the mood to cope with her tantrums.

The morning was well advanced before she had time to think about her mail, which normally consisted of bills, circulars and business letters pertaining to the house. This morning, however, had brought three more letters, one from her parents, one from Graham Lord and one from Judith.

She kept Judith's to the last, reading the news from home with a small stab of nostalgia, then she picked up Graham's letter, which was full of cheerful news. He was going into practice with his father at Arndale, and he would welcome an opportunity to speak with her next time she came home. In the meantime he sent his regards to the lucky man who was her husband.

Lucky man, thought Anne wryly, and wondered what Francis would say if he could read the letter.

Judith's letter was strangely unlike herself. She had taken to writing to Anne, pouring out her small worries and troubles on paper, and Anne had encouraged the child, feeling that Judith needed a sympathetic ear. But now she found Judith's letter stilted, full of awkward little sentences. She would be coming home soon for the long holidays.

Was that what was worrying the child? wondered Anne. Perhaps she was worried about coming home. Anne frowned and remembered the slightly frightened look which had come into the girl's eyes now and again. She had hoped it was only a temporary thing, usual in a young girl growing up when all sorts of fear and imaginations could intrude into her well-ordered life.

Now Anne began to look forward to having Judith home. At least she was happy to have her here . . . or could the stilted letter mean that Judith, too, was now fighting shy of her?

Anne sighed and laid her letters aside, then looked at her notebook to see if there was anything which required her attention. Francis had asked her to see Tom Hansett regarding the hiring of some odd-job men to help with repairs to the greenhouse, and some fencing round the estate. Last week a flock of sheep had strayed on to the lawn, and had eaten up some of their more colourful flowers before being driven back out into their field. The lawn had become pitted with their small hooves and Tom Hansett had not been at all pleased. He had tried to repair the fence, but had found it a bigger job than he anticipated.

Now Anne slipped on her cardigan and made her way to the greenhouse where she knew she would probably find Tom working among some of his more exotic plants. Ever since he had watched her, admiringly, as she arranged flowers for the house, using a variety of containers, and chicken-wire secured with plasticine, or pin-holders and Oasis, he had been fascinated by how beautiful his flowers could look after Anne had completed her arrangements. It had encouraged Tom to look after his more exotic plants, and to help Anne choose the choicest blooms for indoor decoration.

Now she walked into the greenhouse with a pencil and pad in her hand, smiling at the tall genial man who was snipping suckers off a vine.

'No flowers today, Tom,' she assured him, 'though I shall want plenty of blooms when the drawing room is finished.'

She remembered that it might take longer for the drawing room to be back in service than she had hoped.

'I . . . I was sorry about the trouble,

ma'am,' Tom said slowly, as though reading her mind.

'Yes, Tom, I was very careless,' she said, as evenly as she could. 'Now, with regard to the repairs, could I have a complete list, and we'll hire a firm to come and do them all at the same time.'

'Very good,' Tom told her, and began to go over everything with her, recommending a firm which could do the work.

Anne noted it all down competently, then turned to smile at Tom, saying she would put the work in hand straight away. On impulse she decided to walk back to the house via the stables, and as she neared the house she suddenly heard voices and looked round rather bewildered, until she realised she was near the back of the house where the young groom, David Mellor, was standing by an open window talking to Caroline Cook.

'I must see you, Caroline,' he was saying, in a low urgent voice.

'No.'

'But I must talk to you. Surely you can see . . . '

The voice faded and Anne took an uncertain step, wondering how to get back into the house without making her presence known. She liked young David Mellor and didn't want to embarrass him unduly. Was he, perhaps, interested in Caroline?

'No!'

Anne could hear Caroline's soft voice coming even more firmly. A moment later David had almost blundered into her, his face flushing scarlet at the sight of her.

'Oh, sorry . . . I'm so sorry, Mrs. Wyatt,' he apologised. 'I . . . I didn't see you there.'

'How could you?' she smiled. 'I've only just come.'

He looked relieved and apologised again, awkwardly. As she went on towards the kitchen door, she looked up at the morning room window and saw that it had been closed, firmly. Anne walked on into the kitchen thoughtfully.

How well did David Mellor know Caroline? Probably very well. They were of an age, and both had lived near each other all their lives.

Then Anne shrugged off her speculations. She had enough to worry about without adding on David Mellor.

There was Helen, who still seemed to be infatuated by Roger Baxter, and was still determined to keep him apart from her family. Then there was Mrs. Wyatt whose natural taste had to be thwarted for the good of the old Hall. Anne's mind switched to Judith, who seemed so nervous and uncertain of herself, and lastly there was Francis . . . and Caroline Cook, whom she herself had brought into close contact with him, no doubt unwisely for the sake of all three of them.

She felt as though she were being propelled along a dangerous road by some sort of non-stop vehicle, and she had no idea how to get off, or how to stop before they were all injured by collision.

She was about to go upstairs when Caroline called to her, and Anne turned to see her standing in the open doorway of the morning room.

'Could you approve a colour I would like to use?' asked Caroline. 'As you see, the original is unrecognisable, but I rather think it might have been a dark shade of green . . . like this.'

She looked up at Anne, her lovely dark eyes questioning.

'Green looks beautiful,' she said slowly. 'I trust your judgement, Caroline.'

The girl flushed and Anne thought she caught a sudden flash of tears in her eyes.

'I . . . I don't want to usurp your authority,' she said, in a low voice. 'Sometimes . . . sometimes I can't help listening to my own feelings.'

'I'm sure your own feelings will be a good guide,' Anne assured her, and turned away.

It was only later, when the conversation returned to her in full clarity, that

163

she realised Caroline might have been referring to something quite different.

* * *

That evening Francis came home late, and Anne ordered a light supper for him. Mrs. Wyatt had asked Helen to take her to see an old friend living nearby, and they hadn't yet come home.

'It's late for Mother,' Francis frowned, glancing at the clock. 'She usually goes to bed early.'

'It will do her good to get out,' Anne told him. 'She stays in far too much. It isn't good for her to be here all the time.'

He darted a shrewd glance at her.

'What about you?' he asked. 'Do you want to get out more? Shall I make time to give you a better social life?'

'No, of course not . . . not at the moment,' she assured him. 'I realise how busy you are, and there's much to be done here in the house. In a month

164

or two, though, perhaps . . . '

She thought of ways to take a break, and remembered her letters.

'Perhaps I could go home for a few days. I had a letter from Mother today, and one from Graham. He's going into general practice with his father. It . . . it would be nice to see them all again,' she finished, rather lamely.

Again it seemed as though a shutter had come over his face.

'You aren't imprisoned here, Anne,' he told her coldly. 'By all means go and visit your parents whenever you wish. And Graham,' he finished curtly. 'Only I'd have supposed . . . '

'Supposed what?'

'Supposed that now you are married to me, you wouldn't be so ready to run back to see Graham Lord.'

'He's my friend!' she cried, stung. 'When we parted, we said we would always be friends. Graham . . . well, he understands.'

'And I don't!'

'Not much,' she told him honestly. 'I

can't talk to you like I can to Graham.'

'Am I such an ogre?'

She eyed him thoughtfully.

'Sometimes I can't approach you. It's as if . . . as if . . . '

'There's a barrier between us?'

She nodded.

'It keeps coming up. I . . . we . . . can't seem to break it down.'

He said nothing, and she had never felt the barrier more real than it was now. She had no idea why she had told him all this, except that it had been some sort of appeal to change things between them. But now she saw that she had just made things worse.

That night she went once again to the dressing room, but he came up and stood looking down at her as she brushed her hair.

'I asked you to try to make a go of our marriage,' he told her flatly. 'I asked you to meet me half-way, but instead you . . . you're locking yourself into your own small world and shutting me out. You said you'd try, Anne.'

166

Her honey-gold hair lay soft against her pink cheeks, but she was unaware of its gleaming brightness.

'There are some things which need love . . . love on both sides,' she said, in a low voice.

She had made a small floral arrangement for the bedside table, and he selected a golden yellow carnation, almost as bright as her hair. She watched while he twirled it round, then crushed the petals between his fingers.

'Very well, Anne, if that's how you feel.'

The door closed with a quiet click which was more final than a loud bang.

★ ★ ★

Next morning Anne found that Francis had left for Carlisle before she got downstairs, and Mrs Hansett eyed her searchingly and a trifle disapprovingly.

'I think the trip to America has tired Mr. Francis, or something,' she

167

remarked, clearing away his breakfast plates which he had obviously barely touched. Anne said nothing, knowing how much the housekeeper loved Francis. He had been left in her care many times as a boy, and she was fiercely protective towards him.

'Er . . . will Caroline Cook be here for very long, ma'am?' Mrs. Hansett enquired, in a rather strained voice which told Anne that she had practically forced herself to ask the question. Jessie Hansett wasn't one to give way to curiosity, or to interfere in things which didn't concern her.

'A few weeks, then she'll be going to London,' she said quietly.

'Hm. Perhaps the tapestries would have been best left as they were,' remarked Mrs. Hansett gruffly, and again Anne was surprised. The housekeeper had been greatly relieved to see all the restoration work at the old hall.

Anne looked at the older woman's closed face, and knew full well that she, too, did not approve of having Caroline in the house.

'Why do you say that?' she asked bluntly, but already Mrs. Hansett was obviously deciding she had said too much.

'I'm sorry,' she said stiffly. 'It's none of my business, only Mr. Francis . . . she upsets him.'

Anne sat down and poured herself a cup of coffee and Mrs. Hansett hovered nearby.

'He was happy . . . when he brought you home, I mean, ma'am,' she said in a small rush. 'He hasn't always been happy.'

Anne wanted to ask questions, but felt as though her tongue was tied. Had he actually been engaged to Caroline Cook, and if he had, what had happened between them?

'I'm sure he's only a little tired at the moment, Mrs. Hansett,' she said soothingly. 'As you noticed, he needs a rest after his trip to America.'

The woman said nothing more,

169

though Anne could feel her disapproval again, as she refused anything but toast and coffee.

'It's to be hoped Miss Helen isn't off *her* food,' she remarked, and picked up the coffee pot, saying she would make more fresh coffee.

Anne was glad there had been no further searching look, as she was becoming convinced about something which had only been a suspicion for several days. The thought of breakfast was repugnant to her, though she drank the coffee gratefully.

In view of the fact that all was not well with her marriage, Anne thought deeply about the possibility of a coming baby. Her throat tightened a little, thinking how wonderful such news might have been if theirs had been a normal marriage. As it was, she had no doubt Francis would be delighted at the prospect of a family, and would want to protect her and shower her with whatever love he was capable of giving her. She could become important to him for their baby's sake.

But did she want that sort of relationship? It was almost like buying his love, love which might still belong to Caroline Cook.

Anne looked up as Helen came to join her.

'You look on top of the world,' her sister-in-law greeted her, and Anne flushed, knowing very well that her pale face and shadowed eyes told their own tale.

'So do you,' she countered.

'Can we have one more for dinner tonight?' asked Helen, an impish look in her eyes. 'I'd like you all to meet Roger. Will Francis be home on time?'

'I've no idea,' said Anne quickly, and watched Helen raise her eyebrows again.

'Oh, so it's like that, is it?'

'Like what?'

'Having a tiff already.'

'Don't be silly,' said Anne, nerves making her feel irritated.

Then she pulled herself together. It

would be a good thing if Helen did bring Roger Baxter home. She had worried about the girl now and again. There was something very young and appealing about her, in spite of her air of being able to take care of herself.

Anne managed to smile.

'I'm sure we'll all be pleased to welcome Mr. Baxter,' she said gently. 'I'll have a word with Mrs. Hansett. Is there anything you'd like particularly for dinner?'

'The works,' said Helen grandly. 'He's important to me, Anne, don't forget that. I want you all to get to know him, because . . . well, for a very special reason.'

Anne considered this as she looked uncertainly at the girl. This request to bring Roger Baxter home to dinner didn't surprise her. She had been expecting something of the kind. But the look in Helen's eyes was a puzzle as though there was something behind it all which she was missing.

Sighing, she rose. She would never

understand this family, she told herself.

'I'll see to it,' she said to Helen. 'Don't worry, we'll give him 'the works', as you call it.'

'Thanks, Anne,' said Helen, her eyes still dancing. 'I knew you would.'

★　★　★

After the initial questioning look in Mrs. Hansett's eyes, the housekeeper became practical, and she and Anne soon worked out a menu for dinner that evening. Anne thought she had better ring Francis and warn him, also let her mother-in-law know. No doubt for once Mrs. Wyatt would be down in plenty of time for dinner. She would be more eager than anyone to make the acquaintance of Roger Baxter.

'Miss Cook wanted a word with you again, ma'am,' Mrs. Hansett told her, before they parted. 'I think she's having difficulty with that old bed quilt.'

'It's a very beautiful bed quilt,' said Anne. 'Well worth preserving. I'll see

173

her in a moment.'

Meantime she could ring Francis and tell him about Helen's invitation to Roger Baxter. No doubt Francis would be annoyed that Helen had not asked them first of all.

But Anne remembered saying that they would be happy to see him any time, eager as she was to meet the man who was obviously becoming so important to her sister-in-law. Now Helen had taken her at her word! Was that what had caused the gleam of mischief in her eyes? wondered Anne.

When she got through to the office in Carlisle, it was Louise Dalton who answered the telephone.

'Mr. Wyatt is out at the moment, Mrs. Wyatt,' Miss Dalton told her. 'Shall I leave a note for him to ring you back?'

Anne thought for a moment.

'No, I'll leave a message,' she decided. 'Just tell him that Miss Helen has invited a guest for dinner this evening.'

'And you'll want him home early,' said Miss Dalton, a smile in her voice. 'All right. Leave it to me. I'll see he gets home in good time.'

'Thank you,' said Anne, and put down the receiver. Would Francis appreciate being rushed home like that? she wondered. Then she sighed. Oh well, she didn't know what else she could have done. How much easier it would be to run Elvan Hall, she thought as she made her way to the small room where Caroline Cook would be working, if only she did not have to deal with conflicting personalities.

Caroline Cook looked up, her dark eyes brightly beautiful, as Anne walked into the room.

'Hello, Caroline,' she said cheerfully, though she did not feel comfortable in the girl's presence these days. She felt herself to be in a decidedly difficult position over Caroline, feeling that if she asked the girl to leave without being able to say that her work was inferior, then she would be acknowledging to everyone that she was afraid of her.

But if there had been a strong love between Caroline and Francis, surely the girl would wish to go of her own accord. Surely she wouldn't stay here, seeing Francis daily, and knowing that he was married to someone else.

'It's this material, Mrs. Wyatt,' the girl said, picking up the lovely old quilt. 'It's badly tattered and I just can't match it . . . and anything else would look awful.'

Anne bent over the quilt.

'Yes . . . yes, I can see that,' she said thoughtfully.

She looked at the colour which was an unusual shade somewhere between gold and yellow, and wondered if it had come from a ball gown, perhaps worn with excitement and gaiety in a bygone age. There were trunks containing old clothes which she still had to sort out. There might be something among them . . .

'Can you leave it for a day or two?'

she asked. 'I'm going to sort through some old trunks. I may find something.'

'Of course,' said Caroline, her eyes large and wistful as she slanted a glance at Anne. 'It must be nice to be able to do that . . . go through the trunks, I mean . . . have the right to.'

Anne looked at the girl, seeing the eyes become guarded again, and felt a stab of irritation.

'Are you happy here, Caroline?' she asked bluntly. 'Perhaps you'd prefer us to have the rest of the needlework done elsewhere.'

Immediately the dark eyes were widely innocent.

'Oh no, Mrs. Wyatt! You must know how much I enjoy doing this work. I only meant that it must be exciting to dip into old chests and things . . . '

Anne nodded, though she knew that wasn't what Caroline had meant at all. She'd been quietly reminding Anne that it might have been *her* right.

'That's all right, then,' said Anne briskly.

'I was thinking that since there's a lot to do, I could either come earlier or leave later,' Caroline offered diffidently.

'Whatever you like,' agreed Anne. 'You know best how long the job will take.'

The girl's face lit up with a smile, her eyes candid.

'That's all right, then.'

Anne left her to her sewing, thinking that it was nice to find a girl who loved her work so much that she was willing to work longer hours to do the job properly.

And with more opportunity of seeing Francis, said her suspicious mind. Francis had not been at all pleased to see Caroline, but as he got used to her presence, perhaps that would change. Anne rubbed her forehead, feeling that she was becoming more and more involved in making mistakes.

She met Helen in the corridor.

'I'm just going to ask Caroline if she can come for dinner, too, this evening,' she said breezily. 'That is, if you don't mind, Anne. I want Roger to meet all my friends.'

'Oh.'

Anne felt taken aback, though common sense told her that there was no reason why Helen shouldn't invite Caroline.

'You don't mind?'

'Of course not,' she said, her voice rather uncertain, and Helen looked at her with dancing eyes.

'That's all right, then. That will make six, just right for a dinner party.'

Anne thought of Mrs. Wyatt and wondered what she would have to say with, according to her, three undesirables at her table!

★　★　★

Anne didn't feel at her best as she prepared for Helen's guests that evening. Francis had come home early, and she had hurried to meet him, hoping that there would be the old comradeship between them, if nothing else. She could have done with his support. But when she explained about Helen's invitation to her friends, he looked rather cold.

'She shouldn't spring these things on you, Anne,' he told her. 'You must see that Helen consults you first of all.'

'She's entitled to bring her friends home. I like her to do that.'

'Yes, but not to invite them before she asks you.'

'She asked me before she invited Caroline.'

This time she saw his mouth tighten.

'Very well, Anne. So long as you're happy. It's just that I don't want her imposing on you.'

He eyed her intently, and she flushed, well aware of her own pale face and shadowed eyes.

'You look tired, my dear. Sometimes I feel very selfish to . . . to expect so much from you.'

She said nothing, flushing under his scrutiny.

'I . . . I've brought you a necklace to

wear. It belonged to my grandmother. Mother never cared for it, so we kept it in the bank.'

Anne gasped a little when Francis returned with a black case, snapping open the lid to reveal a heavy Victorian necklace of gold set with rubies and diamonds.

She could imagine that the ornate setting would not be to Mrs. Wyatt's liking, since the older woman preferred pretty things, and Anne herself was not sure that she liked it. Francis had fastened it about her neck, and suddenly her plain gold silk dress looked regal and elegant.

She had flushed at his touch, and the warmth of colour in her cheeks made her look beautiful as her long honey-coloured hair was swept back off her forehead.

'It's beautiful,' she said softly, seeing the stones gleam with fire as they caught the light.

She felt his hands tighten on her shoulders, then he turned away.

'That's all right, then. I . . . er . . . I don't know much about these things . . . what you like to wear, I mean.'

He handed her the box awkwardly, and she took it, suddenly wishing she could put her arms round his neck and kiss him for the gift, as could any other wife. But already Francis was turning away, and she looked at her watch. Helen was already downstairs, watching out for Roger Baxter. She, too, was looking her best tonight in a sea blue brocade dress which showed off her tall slender figure and bright pretty face to perfection.

* * *

Anne hadn't known what to expect, but nothing had quite prepared her for her first meeting with Roger Baxter. As Helen led him forward to meet her family, Anne thought he was surely the most handsome man she had ever seen. He was so self-assured and beautifully dressed that almost from the first moment he seemed to take charge of the family party.

Anne glanced at her mother-in-law, a trifle amused to see that for once Mrs. Wyatt seemed at a loss for words.

Francis had welcomed the new arrival cordially, though there was a searching look on his face when he looked at his sister's face. Anne felt suddenly protective towards Helen. She felt that the girl needed someone of her own, and needed the love of a good man with whom she could be happy. She had not exactly gone out of her way to be welcoming to Anne, but she didn't blame Helen for that. There was something vulnerable about her sister-in-law, thought Anne, as she looked round her assembled family, and she wanted to take hold of her and ask her not to lose her heart so wholeheartedly to Roger Baxter, because this polished, very self-assured man was so wrong for Helen. Anne could feel it instinctively, and wanted to protect her from the hurt which surely lay ahead.

A glance at Francis told her he was thinking much the same thing, but a moment later Caroline arrived, and new introductions were made.

Caroline looked breathtaking lovely in a dress she must have made herself, though it was one of the loveliest dresses Anne had ever seen. It was made of black satin, heavily embroidered with gold thread and appliquéd gold kid. With it she wore pretty gold sandals and a narrow bracelet. There was no need for any jewellery, and Anne was suddenly conscious of the heavy weight of the ornate necklace which Francis had given her.

It wasn't a very happy evening. Helen had soon sensed that her mother and Francis were bored with Roger Baxter's monologue regarding business deals in which he shone successfully, and her pride in him was almost theatrical and rather embarrassing.

'I think it's marvellous that you're so successful these days when everything is ten times more difficult, Roger,' she enthused. 'Don't you think so, Francis?'

'Quite,' Francis told her briefly, and refused to make any more comment.

'I think one has to expand one's gifts,' Roger told them expansively. 'Mine just happens to be making the most of whatever I undertake to do. It's a great pity, for instance, that you don't try to make capital out of this old place. Turn it into a hotel, or a rest centre or something. People would pay a fortune to make use of it.'

Mrs. Wyatt was regarding him sourly.

'And those horses of yours, Helen . . . you could offer riding and pony-trekking. Don't you agree, Mrs. Wyatt?'

He looked straight at Anne, as though asking her to side with him, both being on the outside of this family.

'As it happens, I don't, Mr. Baxter,' she told him evenly. 'I feel that there are plenty of hotels already offering all the facilities you suggest. I prefer that Elvan Hall should remain exactly as it is.'

'Oh, but surely . . . what about you,

Miss Cook? Don't you see the possibilities here?'

Caroline had spent most of the evening with her eyes straying to Francis. Now she coloured violently and jumped a little.

'Er . . . I really don't know, Mr. Baxter,' she said primly. 'Only if Francis wanted it that way.'

Mrs. Wyatt gave a snort.

'I'm afraid you'll get no support here, Mr. Baxter,' she said heavily. 'I doubt if even Helen would agree with you.'

'Why not?' demanded Helen, laughing gaily. 'Roger would do it all so well that the place would be made to pay with no loss of comfort to ourselves, I'm sure.'

Suddenly Francis frowned.

'You haven't any ideas . . . business ideas . . . which include Elvan, have you, Mr. Baxter?' he asked flatly, and the other man flushed and, for once, was slightly disconcerted.

'Why, of . . . of course not. It's your home,' he assured them.

186

Anne looked at him speculatively. She had understood why Helen had apparently become so infatuated with him, but not his interest in a girl like Helen. Could it be that he was using her to worm his way into the Hall, which must be a very desirable site in the area? Property development was one of Roger Baxter's pursuits.

But already he had turned the conversation and Helen was once again hanging on his words as he told them an amusing tale from one of his other business deals.

Anne looked for an opportunity to withdraw from the table. Mrs. Wyatt looked tired and Anne felt, for the first time, a warmth of affection for her. The older woman irritated her, and insulted her, but there were points on which they were at one, and ranging themselves against this polished, rather brash man was one of them.

Caroline Cook's presence, too, hadn't helped. The girl was so quiet, her devotion to Francis so apparent that

187

Anne felt embarrassed and uncomfortable, and still at a loss to know what to do about it. She could see the now familiar inscrutable look on Francis' face when his glance rested on Caroline whose beautiful face was an attraction for all eyes, thought Anne wistfully. Even Roger Baxter had looked at the girl with open admiration.

'Will you freelance, Miss Cook?' he was asking. 'When you're fully trained, I mean?'

Caroline flushed.

'It would have been nice, but . . . but one needs capital. A panel, for instance, can cost a great deal of money. Gold thread comes from France, and really *is* made of gold. I'd have to lay out a great deal in materials before selling.'

'Give me your address,' Roger said expansively. 'I'll see what I can do for you.'

Helen threw a rather startled glance at Caroline.

'Caroline's going to London,' she

said quickly, 'doing a post-graduate course.'

'Then I'll have your London address, too, Miss Cook,' Roger Baxter told her, and turned to smile into Helen's eyes. Anne could feel the impatience in Francis, no doubt longing to shake his sister.

That evening, after Anne had seen her guests off the premises, she climbed the stairs thankfully. Roger Baxter had driven Caroline home, after a warm goodnight to Helen, and Mrs. Wyatt had already excused herself and gone upstairs.

'Come and see me before you go to bed, Francis,' she commanded, and he nodded briefly.

He was still with his mother when Anne began to unfasten the heavy Victorian necklace, though the catch was a complicated one, and she found it difficult to undo. As she heard him walk into the bedroom, she opened the dividing door and walked in.

'I can't undo the necklace, Francis.'

He looked at her with bright hard eyes, and turned her round to undo the clasp.

'Couldn't you have stopped her?' he asked abruptly.

Anne's eyes widened.

'I have no control or authority over Helen,' she said defensively. 'She chooses her own friends.'

'Ah yes . . . Helen,' he repeated, and suddenly Anne's eyes grew thoughtful. Had he been referring to Caroline, not to Helen?

'Does it really upset you . . . having Caroline here, I mean? Were you going to marry her, Francis?'

'Who told you that?'

'Helen.'

'Helen seems to be showing remarkably little common sense. I've never discussed my personal affairs with Helen.'

Nor was he discussing them with her, thought Anne wearily. Yet what could he say? That he had married her after a misunderstanding with Caroline, which might have been patched up?

'Try to make her see that she's making a fool of herself,' Francis told her, a hand on her shoulder.

'Who?'

'Helen, of course.'

'Hadn't you better speak to her?' asked Anne.

'Perhaps.'

Suddenly there was tension between them, and a queer sort of shyness. Anne, for a moment, wondered if she ought to tell him about the baby. Then Francis looked at her awkwardly.

'You must be tired,' he said, quite gently.

'Yes . . . yes, I am rather tired,' she admitted, and saw that her room door still stood open.

'Goodnight,' she said, and walked towards it.

'Goodnight,' he echoed, and came to shut the door for her, gently but firmly.

Anne felt that she was being shut

into a box, where she could only live within herself. It was lonely in that box, and she felt even more lonely in her marriage than she had ever felt before.

8

Over the next two weeks, Anne had little time for brooding. The drawing room was finished, though the part of the panelling from which the paint had been removed would not look the same for some time, and Anne had cleverly managed to conceal most of it.

Mrs. Wyatt looked rather sourly at the finished work, and remarked that they need not have bothered to do any painting to the room in the first place. There was absolutely no difference in the drawing room from what it had been before.

Anne bit back an angry retort, as the room was now quite beautiful, and warmly welcoming, thanks to her own efforts.

'It looks wonderful,' Francis told her, putting an arm round her to hold her close.

'I'm glad you're pleased,' she told him, rather awkwardly and shyly.

Helen was spending more and more of her free time in Carlisle, no doubt with Roger Baxter, but Judith came home from school, and Anne warmly welcomed the young girl.

Mrs. Wyatt, too, was obviously delighted to have her youngest daughter home, and Anne saw that she had been wrong about one thing. She really loved this child.

'You're too thin, Judith dear,' she decided.

'I agree,' said Anne, even though her opinion had not been asked. She was concerned to see the little girl looking pale and strained, and wondered if there was anything at school which would be troubling her.

'Are you finding lessons difficult, dear?' she asked gently, when she got the child on her own.

At first there was no answer, but Anne decided to be firm and repeat the question.

'Er . . . lessons?' asked Judith, starting guiltily. 'No, they're O.K., most of them.'

Anne looked searching, then sighed. There had been no hesitation in Judith's voice as she answered, and it certainly wasn't school which was bothering her. Surely it couldn't be her mother, wondered Anne a day or two later. Anne was realising now that Mrs. Wyatt enjoyed having the child with her, but Judith was at her most nervous state when Mrs. Wyatt was calling to her to fetch and carry.

'I think she needs a holiday,' Anne said firmly to Francis.

'She's going to France with Mother in August,' Francis told her. 'Helen was supposed to be going, too, but she wants to opt out . . . no doubt because of that Baxter chap.'

Francis did not like Roger Baxter, and made no secret of this to Anne.

'I mean a rest, then,' Anne pursued. 'Look, Francis, I . . . I'd like to go home for a few days next week. If you

195

remember, I said before that I would try to arrange to go soon. Couldn't I take Judith with me?'

'That will be up to Mother,' he told her. 'I leave her to deal with holidays and off-time for Judith.'

'And I think you should take more interest in her.'

'Interest!' Francis turned to her quickly. 'I love Judith — surely you can recognise that? I thought all women can recognise love when they see it.'

Anne refused to rise to the bait.

'You can love her, but still neglect her. She's not happy. She's too close to you and your mother for you to see it.'

'She's only unsettled because she's separated from all her best friends at school. Young girls like Judith moon about when they have no friends to play with.'

Anne shook her head thoughtfully.

'She doesn't moon about. She's worried about something.'

'About what?'

'I don't know.'

'All right,' he said slowly. 'Get her away, Anne. If you feel she's not herself, I . . . we'll be very grateful to you if you put it right.'

He came to stand beside her.

'I . . . I'll miss you, Anne. Don't stay away long, will you?'

She felt a queer little ache. Soon she would have to tell him about the baby, but it was still her own secret. She would delay for a little while yet.

'I'll have a word with your mother before I ask Judith, then I'll ring up home.'

'Home?' he repeated, and she coloured.

'Mother and Father,' she amended.

★   ★   ★

But Mrs. Wyatt wouldn't hear of Judith going to Arndale with Anne.

'Her holiday is already arranged,' she announced imperiously. 'There's really no need for her to have an extra one, especially when it's only to a small village in Scotland. She'd probably catch cold or something, and spoil her proper holiday later.'

'Arndale has very good weather, being fairly near the sea,' defended Anne. 'I just thought a rest would do her good.'

'Children of Judith's age don't need a rest. She's just naturally pale. She'll soon have some colour in her cheeks running around here at Elvan.'

Was she trying to deceive herself, wondered Anne, or was Mrs. Wyatt so wrapped up in herself, surrounding herself in pretty things and indulging herself in everything she could want, to worry about anyone else? She loved Judith, and obviously wanted her to hand as well.

'It wouldn't do her any harm,' she said mildly, 'and . . . and I'd like to see my parents again. They'll be moving soon and it seems a good time to go at the moment, before we start on the plans for another room.'

A gleam of mischief came into the

older woman's eyes, making her surprisingly like Helen.

'And you don't worry whether I shall carry out my own ideas while you're away?'

'If you did, I'm sure they would be in perfect keeping with the house,' Anne told her smoothly. 'I think you were glad to see the panelling restored again, and that your desire to see it painted was only a whim, one no doubt thwarted in the past.'

The bright eyes gleamed for a moment.

'Perhaps you're right, Anne,' sighed Mrs. Wyatt. 'I shouldn't be feeling old at my age while I'm still in my fifties, but sometimes I do. I feel old at the moment.'

Anne decided that her mother-in-law took far too little exercise and ate far too many sweet things.

'A walk round the garden each day would do you lots of good,' she ventured tentatively. 'You should go out more, visit your friends . . . '

'I get enough exercise walking round Cockermouth,' Mrs. Wyatt said, suddenly petulant again. 'Anyway, I think you ought to ask Francis to accompany you, not Judith, when you go to visit your parents.'

Anne flushed. If only Francis could go home with her! They had been happy at Arndale, or at least she had been happy for a little while. But he was busy, and she was afraid of her mother's sharp eyes, seeing them together, and suspecting that there was a barrier between them.

Was her desire to take Judith partly to serve her own ends, wondered Anne uncomfortably, and to focus the attention of her parents on the young girl? Then she pulled herself together and turned away from the window to face Mrs. Wyatt. It was no use. She didn't really feel happy about Judith.

'Can't you get her doctor to check her over?' she asked. 'I think she's run down.'

'I have little faith in doctors since

Henry died,' said Mrs. Wyatt. 'He seemed just to slip through their fingers.'

Anne again felt sympathy for her mother-in-law. It must have been difficult for her to pick up the threads of her life again after losing a husband who must have been a very strong character. Often Anne could still feel his influence on the old house, and wondered about Francis's relationship with his father. Could it be that the feeling of uncertainty regarding his private life that she had sensed in him was born through being emotionally curbed as a child?

'I'll think it over . . . about Judith,' Mrs. Wyatt told her, an impatient note creeping in.

'Oh, all right,' agreed Anne. 'Perhaps that would be best.'

She put on her coat and decided to go for a walk along the river bank to walk off her irritation. Why should Mrs. Wyatt be so difficult over an invitation which was born out of concern for

201

Judith? She ought to be grateful that Anne wanted to take the child home, and that her parents would welcome the little girl. Surely this wasn't another oblique way of trying to make her feel inferior! Lately she had been feeling that the older woman was beginning to accept her.

Anne hunched up her shoulders and strode on, and a minute later her heart bounded as she heard the baying of hounds and watched the approach of several men in sporting clothes who were bent on following the pack.

Anne was now used to fox-hunting, although she did not care for it, but otter-hunting was another matter and she ran forward and demanded to know where they had come from and what authority they had to be there.

'You're trespassing on our land,' she told them furiously. 'I will not have the otters hunted here! There are far too few already . . . practically none at all.'

'They're destructive.'

A man stepped forward to defend his

sport, but Anne was too angry to listen. 'Go . . . all of you!' she ordered. 'You have no right here!'

Anger had given her authority, though deep down she wondered if she was in the wrong. They had come from another county and were no doubt entitled to cross boundaries if they had raised an otter.

She watched them go, then turned back home, a wretched feeling of sickness gnawing at her again.

'What was that?' asked Mrs. Wyatt, who had heard the commotion.

'Otter-hunters,' Anne told her, her eyes still sparking dangerously. 'I stopped them, if you must know.'

She waited for the usual rather contemptuous lecture, but for once it didn't come.

'Good for you,' approved Mrs. Wyatt. 'I hate the otters being hunted. And Anne, you can take Judith, if your parents wish to offer her hospitality.'

Anne's anger dissolved and a smile spread over her face.

'Thank you,' she said simply. 'I'm certain Judith will benefit from the change.'

As she walked on into the house, she was unaware that the older woman was looking after her, a strangely soft expression on her face.

★   ★   ★

Judith looked better already when Anne began to make arrangements to take her to Arndale the following Monday. A telephone call to her parents had ensured that they were both expected, and a room prepared for the little girl.

'Won't Francis be with you?' asked Mrs. Drummond, rather anxiously. 'I was looking forward to having you both home for a few days.'

'He's very busy at the moment,' said Anne quickly. 'It's an American contract. It will have to be dealt with carefully.'

'I understand,' said Mrs. Drummond, who didn't at all. Surely Francis would find it was as easy to come to Arndale as to go home to Elvan Hall from Carlisle? Still, it would be nice to meet Anne's young sister-in-law.

Judith took the news that she was invited to Anne's home in Scotland rather quietly, but she felt the little girl was happy about the prospect of an unexpected holiday, and she encouraged her to make her own preparations.

As far as Anne was concerned, there was only one loose string to be tied up, and that was Caroline Cook. Mrs. Wyatt had been blunt that she did not want Caroline still 'mooning around' while Anne was away.

'The girl's got no pride,' she said roundly.

'I think you're wrong about her,' said Anne. 'She's really very pleased to have this job to do. She loves the work and it must be excellent experience for her.'

'A fat lot you know,' her mother-in-law informed her. 'I tell you, she's hanging on with all her pretty kitten claws.'

'But . . . but Francis and I are married. What you suggest is too ridiculous.'

'People don't always stay married. Her cousin got a divorce from her husband last year and has married someone else. She's seen it happen before.'

Again uncertainty gripped Anne, and a day or two before she and Judith were due to leave from Arndale, she went to see Caroline in the morning room.

'Can I interrupt you to talk for a moment?' she asked, sitting down.

The small dark girl looked up questioningly.

'Er . . . have you got a great deal more work to get through, Caroline?'

'Not a lot, no. Since you found that material which matched as well as could be expected, I've been able to get on quite quickly.'

'That's good,' said Anne, relieved. 'It's just that . . . well, I shall be going up to my old home for a week or two, in Arndale, and Judith is coming with me.

That means . . .'

'I know what it means,' said Caroline in a low voice. 'It means Mrs. Wyatt won't want me here, when there are mainly just the two of us in the house together. She glared at us just the other day when Francis and I were only just speaking together for a short while.'

So they *did* talk together sometimes, thought Anne. She'd thought Francis rarely saw Caroline.

'Don't worry,' Caroline was saying quickly, 'I can finish, except for a few items which could wait for a while, by tomorrow evening.'

'That will be splendid,' said Anne, rather awkwardly.

Suddenly Caroline put a small hand on her arm.

'I'm sorry,' she said, her eyes beginning to mist over with tears. 'I . . . I should never have come here. It was wrong of me. Only the temptation was too great and I didn't know you were going to be so . . . so good to me.'

Anne began to rise, feeling rather uncomfortable.

'I do love Francis, you see.' Caroline's tears were flowing more freely. 'Helen knows. She's always known. I . . . I thought he loved me. He was always so loving towards me and when I finished college, I . . . I told him I wouldn't mind not doing my post-grad, if he wanted other plans for us. He . . . he sort of . . . changed. I think it was Mrs. Wyatt. She's never liked me because there was some sort of scandal in my grandmother's time.'

Caroline managed a faint smile.

'I may be related to Francis. You never know. Perhaps that's what she has against me, or . . . or she just feels I'm not good enough. But then Francis had married you and I . . . I felt all shattered. I thought it would be me, you see. Even afterwards I thought . . . somehow . . . there must be some mistake.'

Anne sat down, feeling rather faint. She could have dealt with a different sort of girl, but Caroline was soft and gentle, and it looked as though Francis had let her down badly. Anne tried to think of him objectively, wondering if her love for him had blinded her to his true nature. Could he really make promises, then turn away without a word? And why had he then married her? She had no more to offer than Caroline.

She felt her face go cold and clammy, as the blood drained from her cheeks, and Caroline's sudden exclamation of concern.

'Do you feel all right, Mrs. Wyatt?'

Anne nodded weakly.

'Oh dear,' cried Caroline. 'I . . . I shouldn't have said all that. Are you sure you're all right?'

'Yes. Don't worry,' said Anne, fighting off a wave of giddiness.

She heard the other girl's sudden intake of breath.

'You . . . is it a baby?' she whispered.

Anne hesitated and immediately Caroline again began to apologise.

'No, it's all right,' said Anne. 'I know you'll respect my confidence. I rather wanted to keep it to myself for a little while, so I told no one.'

She emphasized the last words, and Caroline nodded, understanding.

'Some people are secretive about . . . about certain things. I find I like to get used to major happenings before I tell anyone else.'

'I understand.'

The girl's tears had vanished and she was looking at Caroline with more reserve.

'Can I ask you to keep my secret and tell no one?' asked Anne.

'Of course. I'm not a tell-tale.'

'I'm sorry,' Anne told her, ashamed. 'I shall see you before I go, but in case we don't have time for a chat, I wish you well in your course. I . . . I'm sorry you've been disappointed, but . . . there's nothing more I can say.'

'Of course not,' said Caroline crisply, as though ashamed of showing her wounded feelings to another girl.

Anne left the room feeling uncomfortable and rather vulnerable. Now she would have to tell Francis, since her secret was no longer entirely hers.

★ ★ ★

But she had no opportunity for a private word with Francis before she and Judith left the following Saturday. He telephoned to say that he was very busy and likely to be late each evening, so he would just stay at the flat which he still kept for emergencies.

'There's something I'd have liked to discuss with you before I left, Francis,' Anne told him slowly.

'But surely you won't be staying away too long?'

'About a couple of weeks.'

There was silence for a moment.

'I'll come home then, Anne, though I may be late, or perhaps you could postpone your visit till Monday? I . . . I thought you were just going for a few days.'

Was he beginning to take her for granted? wondered Anne, still thinking about all Caroline had told her.

'No, it's all right, Francis,' she said briskly. 'It will all keep till we get back. My parents are expecting us on Saturday and Judith is looking forward to it.'

Again there was a short silence.

'And you'll also be seeing Graham Lord?'

This time she couldn't keep the anger out of her voice.

'Most probably. He happens to live in Arndale, and we've been friends since childhood. We . . . we became even better friends when we realised we wouldn't be happy together if we married. Surely you understand that, Francis.'

'Of course,' he told her quickly. 'Have a good journey, Anne. If you need extra money, don't hesitate . . . '

'Thank you, I've quite enough,' said Anne, still feeling annoyed.

She put down the receiver and met

Helen's amused eyes as she came downstairs, having just had a bath and change of clothing.

'Hello, Anne. You and Francis sound rather at odds with one another. Is it a lovers' tiff?'

'Of course not,' said Anne shortly. 'Just making arrangements before I leave with Judith.'

'Oh yes. Can't wait to get away now. Is that it? After rushing to get here, too.'

'Now don't you start, Helen,' said Anne, nettled. 'I'll be jolly glad of the break.'

'Away from us all?' Helen sighed deeply, then her light brittle voice softened. 'I don't blame you, Anne.'

A moment later there was gaiety in her voice again.

'What's the betting I shall be engaged when you get back?'

Anne paused on her way to the stairs. 'To Roger Baxter?'

'Do you think Francis will approve? Or Mother? I have to get their approval, you know.'

Helen's voice hardened.

'In this day and age! They have to okay my husband for me. Daddy saw to that.'

Anne was rather startled as she looked at her sister-in-law curiously.

It hadn't occurred to her that Helen's financial affairs were dependent on Francis and her mother. In fact, she suddenly realised that she knew little about financial arrangements for other members of the family, except that Francis looked after them all at the moment.

'I can please myself at twenty-five, but meantime I'm dependent on Francis,' said Helen heavily. 'But anyway, by twenty-five I shall be half-way towards being an old maid!'

This time Anne laughed. Helen looked much too young and pretty to be looking forward to remaining a spinster.

'You may laugh,' her sister-in-law said, rather crossly, 'but it's not much fun having to win over Mother and

Francis. But I've tried out a plan, and I think it will work. We'll soon see.'

'Don't do anything silly,' said Anne, suddenly alarmed.

She looked at the younger girl, surprised to realise how fond she was of her, even though Helen irritated her at times.

'I'm not as silly as I look,' Helen told her, 'and I know Mother . . . and Francis!' She looked at Anne, her eyes dancing again.

'I think I know why he married you.'

'Why?' asked Anne, before she could stop herself.

'Don't you know? I would have thought you'd know very well why a man asks you to be his wife.'

Helen's laugh was light with amusement and Anne felt cross with her again, and decided that Helen could go and jump in the lake. She irritated her beyond endurance at times. With flags of colour in her cheeks, she climbed the stairs.

9

Anne had to control the sudden rush of tears when she eventually drew up her small white car on the gravel drive in front of her old home. Her mother was already at the door to meet her, and to embrace little Judith who had been very quiet on the journey, though Anne had sensed that she was enjoying the changing scene of the countryside. Now and again she had remarked on an unusual bird, on the beauty of a charming house set into the back-ground of trees and hills, and on lovely flowers growing in a cottage garden.

'I bet you're ready for your tea, my dear,' Mrs. Drummond remarked kindly, her eyes concerned when she saw how slender and frail the child looked.

'I doubt the air around your new abode isn't doing much for either of you,' she remarked, her eyes going shrewdly to Anne's face.

'It's wonderful air,' said Anne rather shortly. There were some things which she didn't want to discuss, even with her mother, just yet.

'We've just had rather a hectic time recently, giving the Hall a face-lift,' she explained more gently, with a smile. 'We'll soon come round after a rest.'

Then Stephen Drummond came out of his study where he had been working on a new book, and welcomed them heartily. Once again Judith shrank a little, but Anne ran forward to hug her father, glancing briefly at her mother. If anyone needed her care, it was Stephen, she thought, with a small pang.

'When do you go to the cottage, Mother?' she asked casually, as she helped to make the final preparations for tea in the kitchen.

'Next month,' Mrs. Drummond told her, 'and don't worry too much about your father. So long as he doesn't have any sudden upset, he'll gradually regain his strength when he gets a long rest. He's just been overworked, that's all. He has two parishes to run and it doesn't give him much free time, hopping from one place to another, and doing his books as well. Er . . . I gather that Francis seems to be keeping busy, too.'

'It's an American contract,' Anne told her briefly. 'He has to look after a great many things to make sure everything is properly done.'

'Then you're happy, dear? You really love Francis?'

'I do love Francis,' she said quietly. 'There's no need to worry, Mummy. It's Judith I want to sort out.Somehow . . . somehow there's something wrong with the child, and I can't think what it can be. I've brought her here to let her roam about in the fresh air for a while, with lots of peace and quiet for her own pursuits, but I mean to keep an eye on her and see how she reacts. If she grows rather more like a girl of her age should be, then I'll know it's something at the

Hall which is responsible . . . or . . . someone.'

'Who?' asked Mrs. Drummond bluntly. 'Who could be a worry to a child like that?'

But Anne felt very reluctant to suspect, even, that it was her mother-in-law. She knew that Mrs. Wyatt deeply loved her youngest daughter, and wouldn't harm her in any way, unless it was something beyond her control.

'I don't know,' she said heavily. 'Let's just see what happens over the next few days. By the way, do you see much of Graham?'

'Not so much.'

This time it was Mrs. Drummond's turn to eye her daughter shrewdly.

'Were you wanting to see him?'

'I only wanted a word with him about Judith,' said Anne calmly, and met her mother's eyes. 'Don't worry, I'm not having any regrets and neither, I'm sure, is he. Are we ready now that I've mixed this salad? I hope Daddy is talking nicely to Judith.'

Mrs. Drummond and Anne walked through to the dining room where Stephen Drummond was proclaiming in his booming voice all about the interesting wild life in the area, while Judith listened in obvious fascination.

'This young lady knows as much about the habits of our wild life as I do,' Mr. Drummond said, turning to Anne with one of his rare smiles.

'We had two roe deer on the lawn yesterday morning,' said Judith eagerly. 'There was a mist off the river when I looked out of my bedroom early, and they were knocking heads together. They then ran off into the woods. Hansett says we must chase them, or they ruin the trees.'

'I didn't notice them,' Anne admitted, sitting down beside Judith. 'Was that before I got up, Judith? Judith?'

But the child had obviously said all she wanted to say at the moment. She didn't answer, and Anne caught her father's eye and shrugged a little. She was getting used to Judith's sudden withdrawals into herself. Later she would see what her father thought of the child.

Over the next few days, Judith ran wild over the big garden, wearing torn jeans and sandals, her hair caught back in a ponytail. Her fair skin became freckled and her body began to look more sturdy as she ate with increasing appetite, but her odd, shy reserve was still much in evidence.

'Have a word with Graham,' Mr. Drummond advised. 'Doesn't her mother feel that a doctor could be consulted?'

'I don't think she wants to recognise that Judith isn't perfectly well, Father,' said Anne slowly, 'and certainly her general health seems good. It's just . . . '

She broke off and her father nodded thoughtfully.

'I know. As though she suddenly shuts herself off from everything. Don't you think she's frightened about something, Anne?'

Anne nodded, wondering what it

could be. There was no sign that Judith was any better here at Arndale than she had been at Elvan.

'Yet she seems happy enough,' she remarked, going to the window where the child was romping with their old spaniel who was still game for a bit of fun which wasn't too strenuous or rough.

'All right, Father, I'll go and see Graham.'

* * *

It was odd meeting Graham again at their old trysting place. Anne had rung him up, hearing the pleasure in his voice when he talked to her again.

'Are you coming over for dinner?' he asked.

'No, Graham. At least, not yet. I've got Judith with me. Look, I want to ask you about something. Could we meet at our old place and I'll tell you all about it?'

Graham's voice had been slightly

cagey when he replied.

'You sound very mysterious, my dear. Is there anything wrong, Anne?'

She laughed.

'Don't get the wind up. I'm not trying to latch on to you again. Have you got a girl-friend likely to object to your meeting me?'

'Dozens,' laughed Graham, 'and I'm keeping it that way for now. What about you, though . . . and Francis?'

'He knows I want to talk to you,' said Anne shortly. 'It's about Judith, his little sister.'

'Ah, I see,' said Graham, obviously relieved, then in turn concerned. 'What's wrong with her?'

'I don't know. That's why I want to talk to you.'

'If it's a medical matter, you should see her own doctor,' said Graham, slightly pompously.

'Oh, Graham, you do sound stuffy,' said Anne, a hint of laughter in her voice.

'Thanks very much. You've wounded

me to death. Will our old place do?'

'Fine,' said Anne. 'Usual time?'

'No, we'll have to make it before surgery. Five o'clock.'

'Five o'clock,' agreed Anne.

Now Graham was sitting on the style waiting for her, but to Anne he seemed very different from the rather untidy boy who had been the friend of her childhood. This Graham was a man who looked much more used to handling responsibility.

Then he turned to smile at her, and Anne ran forward. Automatically Graham jumped down and gave her a bearlike hug.

'It's good to see you again, Anne.'

'Good to see you, too, Graham.'

He had brought his coat and a bar of chocolate and they sat down to eat it together companionably. Though, thought Anne, everything was different. She felt different. She felt older, even, than Graham.

'I've brought Judith up with me,' she explained, telling Graham about her new family.

'She must have been born when her mother was in her forties,' he remarked slowly.

'An afterthought, as Mrs. Wyatt puts it. I know she loves Judith though, Graham. But she *is* inclined to order the child about and shows impatience when Judith appears to be very stupid at times. She's not stupid either, though I don't think her school reports are all that good.'

'I see . . . and you don't want to take her for a normal examination?'

'That's her mother's responsibility, not mine, or Francis'. Only he has such a lot on hand at the moment, and they think I'm just fussing.'

'I see.'

Graham found a blade of grass and began to chew it, as he had done countless times before.

'Suppose I take you both out on Saturday? Where should we go? Sweetheart Abbey?'

'No, not there,' said Anne quickly,

remembering she had gone there on her honeymoon just eight weeks ago. 'Somewhere near the sea — Creetown, perhaps. We'll let Judith play on the rocks by the shore.'

'Will you do the picnic?'

Again Anne laughed and nodded. Graham loved her wholesome sand-wiches.

'Of course. What time can you make it?'

'It will have to be after lunch, around three.'

'We'll be ready,' Anne promised him.

* * *

Anne loved the coastline between Gatehouse-of-Fleet and Creetown, having spent many happy hours there as a child. She hoped for a fine day on Saturday, as the weather had dulled a little during the week, and she had spent her time helping her mother to sort out more of their personal possessions before the move.

'I shall have to find homes for a great many pieces,' Mrs. Drummond sighed regretfully. 'The cottage will never hold all this. I don't suppose you . . . Anne?'

Anne thought for a moment. Elvan Hall was already full of furniture, but it would be nice to have some pieces of her very own. But would Francis welcome extra furniture? Anne brooded, then lifted her chin. It was her home now too, and he could put up with it. She knew she could fit some things in very well.

'I'll be delighted to have them, Mummy,' she agreed, 'and so will Francis, I'm sure.'

'That's good, darling,' said Mrs. Drummond, relieved. 'Some of them have been in your father's family for generations. Perhaps . . . perhaps you can pass them on to your own family, Anne.'

Anne flushed scarlet. Was it showing already? She had found some old dresses in her wardrobe which she had discarded, but which she now found very comfortable, and not at all tight round the middle. In fact, so far she could detect little change.

'It will be a few years before my family will want them, surely,' she said, with a rather forced laugh.

'I was talking about the future,' Mrs. Drummond said quietly.

★ ★ ★

Judith was quite happy to go with Anne and Graham on the picnic. Graham had a way with children, and soon had her laughing merrily as they piled the picnic things into his old car.

'Have you brought a spare dress for her, Anne?' Graham asked, peering in one of the bags. 'She'll fall in the sea, sure as eggs. Every time I get a new girlfriend and take her to the seaside on a picnic, she falls in and I have to bring her home dripping all over my car — like Anne here.'

Anne grinned sheepishly.

'I couldn't do anything else,' she

defended, 'when you blundered into me and pushed me in.'

'Bring a spare frock for you, too, then,' advised Graham. 'I might push you in again!'

Anne could see the child relaxing as they poked fun at one another, then she climbed into the back of the car, having put Judith in the front seat.

Mr. and Mrs. Drummond came to see them off, and Anne turned away as she caught a look of nostalgia on their faces. There was no doubt they would have preferred her to marry Graham, and to have settled down in Arndale. Anne's thoughts turned again to Francis, as they frequently did. Would they ever be really happy together? she wondered.

She remembered how dear and precious he had been to her during their honeymoon, and she had felt then that he had strong feelings for her, even if they weren't the true love she wanted from him.

But now? Now she didn't know any

more. He hadn't liked her close contact with Caroline Cook. Had he really let the girl down, letting her think he loved her, then rejecting her so suddenly? Could she picture Francis doing such a thing?

Yet Caroline was beautiful and talented. She had put her pride in the dust by coming back to the Hall as an employee of Anne's, but real love was stronger than pride, and Anne realised how the girl must have been drawn towards the place. She couldn't help herself.

Yet Francis had hurriedly turned to herself, almost as though he needed their marriage as some sort of protection. Protection? Anne's eyes grew wide as her thoughts raced on. She was aware of Graham talking gaily to Judith in front of her, though again the child was rather silent, and Anne was staring almost unseeingly at the passing countryside. What would happen if Francis no longer needed her? Would he regret being tied to her, and would he insist on keeping those ties when he knew about their baby? He would have to know soon.

Anne looked at Judith's small dark head, knowing that although she had wanted to help the child, she had also wanted to think things out for herself. Somehow she must take hold of herself and re-plan her own life before going back, and without allowing her love for Francis to overrule her common sense.

She came to herself, glancing up at the mirror in the car, to catch Graham's eyes on her briefly.

'Nearly there,' he said. 'You all right, Anne?'

'Of course.'

'Did you remember the mustard?'

'Of course.'

'And hard-boiled eggs?'

'Of course. Judith shelled those.'

'Then I'll throw her into the sea if she's left any shell on the eggs. So just you look out, young lady,' he boomed at her, and Judith smiled back at him, her eyes sparkling as she turned to look back at Anne.

She looks so like Francis at times, thought Anne with a pang. It wouldn't be very easy to make plans objectively.

Anne and Graham had long ago found their favourite picnic spot and he drove there automatically.

'Come on, young lady,' he called to Judith, handing out baskets and rugs. 'We'll eat first. I'm starving!'

Anne spread a red-checked tablecloth and put out plates of sandwiches and cakes, then began to pour out cups of tea for Judith and Graham, and coffee for herself.

Graham had made a place beside him on the rug for Judith to sit down, and she accepted a sandwich, shyly at first, then becoming more relaxed.

'Another sandwich, love?' asked Graham quietly, then lifted the plate when she didn't answer.

'Another sandwich, Judith? Take a good drink of that tea, then let me ask you something.'

'What?' asked Judith.

'How long is it since you found it difficult to hear?'

Anne almost felt herself choke on her own sandwich, and gasped a little as Judith's hand shook, spilling a few drops of tea. Surely . . . surely that wasn't what was wrong! Surely Judith couldn't be deaf?

'Easy now, poppet,' said Graham soothingly, putting down Judith's cup and taking her hands in his. 'There's no need to be frightened of being hard of hearing. It could easily be caused by something which could be put right quite simply, so don't be scared.'

The child raised wide eyes to his face, then glanced fearfully at Anne. Graham had spoken to her slowly and carefully, and she had obviously heard every word.

'I . . . I don't know,' she whispered. 'It just started and . . . and then got worse and . . . and sometimes I didn't hear things at school and missed bits in lessons. And . . . and sometimes I didn't hear Mummy until she shouted at me and thought I was stupid . . . '

The last word was choked back as Judith began to cry quietly. A moment later she was in Anne's arms while the tears came, and Anne's own eyes were distressed as she looked at Graham.

'Let her cry,' he said quietly. 'She's bottled up her fear for too long.'

After a while the little girl blew her nose and Graham again took her hands.

'You know I'm a doctor, Judith, but there are lots better doctors who know all about ears.'

He pulled out his own ears so that he looked like a monkey and the child managed a watery smile, as she nodded.

'Well, we can get one of those doctors to look inside your ears. It may only be wax hardened on as you can still hear fairly well in both ears. Oh yes, I've tested you without your knowing it! So don't go flying into a panic. Why didn't you tell Anne?'

'She'd have told Francis,' said Judith promptly, 'and . . . and . . . '

'Maybe I would,' agreed Anne, 'but it would have been with a view to helping you, darling. Surely you know that.'

'He'd have worried, and . . . and Mummy, too. And I didn't know it could be made better. I . . . I didn't want you all to know in case you were frightened for me, then I'd have been frightened, too.'

'But you aren't now?' insisted Graham.

Judith hesitated.

'I am still . . . a bit,' she admitted honestly.

'Look! Look there,' he said, and turned her round to see one or two tiny bluetits which had come to pick up crumbs Graham had thrown a short distance away.

'They have courage, haven't they, Judith? I mean, for all they know, that bread is a trap so that we can catch them. But they take their tiny lives in their own tiny claws and bravely hop within a few feet of us big giants. They have courage, haven't they?'

Judith nodded.

'All right. I'll try to have courage, too.'

'Good girl! You'll be better than your Uncle Graham, then. You should hear me yell at the dentist's.'

Once again Judith was laughing, this time with more genuine merriment in her voice. She had also regained her appetite and was tucking in, again, to more tea and sandwiches as though a weight had been taken off her mind.

'You can go and play, while Anne and I repack,' Graham told her, and they watched her clamber happily over the rocks while Anne repacked the picnic basket and folded up the tablecloth.

'Oh, Graham,' she said, a small catch in her voice as they loaded the boot of the car, 'I'm frightened now. Suppose . . . suppose she does lose her hearing? I never suspected that was what was wrong.'

'Now don't you panic either,' he told her flatly. 'I bet you anything you like she's got wax hardened in. She can go to her own doctor, and he'll arrange for her to have her ears syringed. No doubt the wax will need to be softened first with oil, if my guess is correct, but even if it's more than that, isn't it better to find out while something can be done?'

'Yes. Yes, of course. I'll have to tell Francis . . . and Mrs. Wyatt.'

'Are you really happy at Elvan?' asked Graham suddenly. 'You don't talk too much about your life there, and very little about Francis. I . . . I'd hate to think I let you go, if it was a mistake and you didn't love him after all.'

'I do love him, Graham, only . . . '

She hesitated. Not even to Graham could she admit that Francis didn't love her.

'Only what?'

'Nothing.'

He was silent for a while.

'And you don't want to tell me anything else?'

She looked at him enquiringly.

'I'm not a doctor for nothing, Anne.'

She coloured guiltily.

'I'm keeping it a secret yet, Graham. I . . . I haven't told Mummy and Daddy.'

'Why not? I would have thought it would be a matter for great jubilation. It could be the son and heir, after all. You haven't even told . . . anybody?'

He emphasised the last word and she shook her head, realising what he meant. He took her hand.

'Nothing worrying you, Anne? Surely you can't be worried about having a baby? It happens all the time.'

Again she shook her head, unable to explain why she hadn't immediately told Francis. She had been vaguely aware of other cars passing on the main road, and occasionally one would stop while someone got out to look at the view. Now she felt Graham's fingers tighten on her own as he looked up, and a moment later Judith rushed past them, scrambling up over the rocks.

'Francis!' she cried. 'Francis! How funny to see you here. We . . . we all thought you were in the office.'

'Obviously,' he said icily, his arms going automatically round his small sister while his eyes went over her head to burn into Anne's. She saw that he was furiously angry.

'F-Francis,' she said, rather weakly. 'How . . . how did you get here? I mean, we came on a picnic . . . with Graham.'

'So I see.'

'Now don't get the wrong ideas, Wyatt,' said Graham hurriedly. 'We're just doing something we've been doing for years. I mean . . . '

Francis' face was hard as granite.

'I called to take you home, Anne. You and Judith.'

'There's something wrong?'

'Very wrong.'

'Not . . . an accident?'

'No. Everyone is perfectly all right as far as health is concerned.'

'Except one,' interrupted Graham, his eyes going to Judith. 'I'm a doctor, Wyatt, and I'd like a word with you.'

'I've no wish to discuss my wife with

you, Lord,' Francis said, glaring.

'But you don't understand', cried Anne. 'We've got something to tell you.'

'I'm sure you have,' he said heavily, while Judith looked from one to the other with large eyes.

'We can't talk here,' Graham said crisply. 'I shall have to see you later, Wyatt. I'm due back for surgery anyway.'

'I'll drive you home, Anne, you and Judith. We'll pick up your things.'

'I don't want to come with you, Francis,' she said coldly. 'You knew I was coming for two weeks. We've only been here for one.'

'I didn't know then what I know now,' he told her, 'though I'd rather not discuss personal matters regarding our family till we're back in our own home.'

Suddenly she understood, seeing a vision of Helen's mischievous face as she offered her a bet that she would be engaged by the time Anne got home. She had probably tackled her mother after Anne left, and Francis had just newly been called in. He disliked Roger Baxter, and Anne knew him well enough now to realise his anger was mainly caused by fear. He wouldn't want his sister messing up her life. Especially when he might have messed up his own, thought Anne miserably.

She knew now why Francis insisted on waiting till they were home before bringing it all out into the open. He couldn't discuss Helen in front of either Graham or Judith.

'We'll go back with Francis,' she told Graham, 'then you can drive straight on to surgery. Thank you for your help, Graham.'

'Best transfer all your picnic stuff, then,' Graham suggested, and there was almost a truce as they transferred hampers and rugs, and installed Judith and Anne in the other car.

'I'll sit in the back this time,' said Judith. 'Francis is awfully angry. He gets angry sometimes, but he soon forgets that he is angry.'

She grinned and Anne saw that she

wasn't afraid of her brother's anger. She saw Graham hurriedly speaking to Francis, his hands waving as though he were explaining something. Francis turned white again, as he looked towards them, and Anne suspected that Graham was telling him about Judith.

A moment later he walked over to his car and climbed in.

'Don't worry, Francis, she'll be all right,' Anne said gently.

He turned to stare at her, a look of pain in his eyes.

'Is Lord still so important to you,' he asked, 'that you should discuss matters with him before me? Does he matter so much to you still, Anne?'

'Of course not . . . at least, not in the way you mean. We've been friends since childhood, though, Francis. It's only natural I should consult him.'

He looked at her for a long time, then drew a hand over his eyes.

'I . . . I've made a mistake some-where, Anne. I've put the wrong things first. But I can't think . . . not till we get home to Elvan. I'm sorry I've lost your trust.'

'But you haven't, Francis!'

Even as she said it, Anne felt her face colour. She *had* doubted her trust in him, especially over Caroline Cook. Somehow he had sensed it. She heard him sigh as she watched the shadows on his face.

'Come on, let's apologise to your parents. I think we need to take Judith home now in any case. At least Lord offers me some hope for her. He thinks her hearing is only slightly impaired by hardened wax, and there's no disease. God grant that he's right. I'm grateful to him, and . . . and I've apologised.'

He had spoken in a low voice so that Anne could hear, but Judith, sitting back behind them, obviously hadn't managed to catch, because she leaned forward.

'What, Francis?'

'We'll sort you out, darling, don't worry.'

'I know, Francis. I was so afraid you'd

be worried, though. You always have so many things to do.'

Anne saw his hands tighten on the steering wheel.

'Too many,' he agreed. 'Too many for my own good.'

Anne said nothing. Soon they would be home and she would have to explain their sudden departure without bringing in Helen's name.

* * *

Anne managed to meet her mother's questioning eyes with a reassuring smile.

'I'm sorry, Mummy darling,' she said brightly. 'I'll have to go home with Francis, and take Judith with me.'

Mrs. Drummond looked disappointed.

'I thought you were concerned for the child's health,' she said bluntly.

'We've got a pointer now,' Anne told her quickly, having sent Judith upstairs to pack her few odds and ends.

244

'Graham has found out she's having difficulty with hearing. The quicker we see about it the better.'

'Oh, poor lamb!' cried Mrs. Drummond, her suspicions vanishing. 'Oh, by all means you must take her home if it means consulting the proper medical authority. Is . . . is it serious, Anne?'

Anne's cheeks were flushed. She hated telling half the truth.

'Graham thinks there's a good chance it can be put right fairly easily,' she said, and glanced at Francis who had been standing rather aloofly. 'I'll just go up and see to Judith's clothes, and mine.'

As she ran upstairs, Francis stepped forward rather awkwardly.

'Thank you for having Judith . . . and Anne.'

'She looks tired, my dear,' his mother-in-law told him bluntly, and he nodded, a trifle withdrawn.

'I hope that's only temporary, Mrs. Drummond. I shall see Mrs. Hansett and arrange for more help for Anne.'

Nell Drummond said nothing, but turned with some relief to her husband who had come in from the garden.

'I'm afraid Anne has to take Judith home, dear. Graham says she must have her hearing tested.'

'Of course . . . that's what it is,' said Mr. Drummond. 'She listened best when I boomed at her. Well, and how are you, Francis, my boy?'

Francis relaxed, and smiled.

'Keeping well, thank you, sir. But you look ready for your move to the cottage, if you don't mind my saying so. Wouldn't you both like to come to Elvan till the cottage is ready for you . . . after you've preached your last sermon, of course.'

'That's very kind of you, Francis,' said Anne's mother, softening.

'We may be glad of that invitation,' Stephen Drummond assured him. 'May we let you and Anne know?'

'Of course.'

Then as he looked up to see Anne coming downstairs with Judith by the hand, Francis seemed to step back into his shell.

'I'll take those cases,' he offered, rather awkwardly.

'Can I take my conch shell?' asked Judith. 'Mr. Drummond said I could have the conch shell on his desk.'

'Very well,' agreed Francis, and the little girl hurried away, while goodbyes were said, rather awkwardly.

Anne climbed into her own small car. Judith was travelling with Francis in the larger one, and Anne was glad to be alone with her thoughts. She felt a rush of love for her parents as she waved them goodbye, following Francis out of the drive. She had their love, which was very precious to her.

She tried to keep up with the car in front, seeing that Francis was deliberately reducing speed to try to keep her in view. At first the roads were very empty, but towards Carlisle traffic intervened, and the bigger car was soon lost, well ahead. When Anne finally arrived at Elvan Hall, it was early evening and the other car was already drawn up outside the front door. She climbed out, still aware of the small thrill she always experienced when she saw the lovely old place in the bright summer evening. There was no doubt that Elvan Hall now held a special place in her heart.

Helen was crossing the entrance hall, but she hurried forward to meet Anne, giving her an unexpected hug.

'Francis had to go upstairs,' she explained, 'and Judith is with Mother. It's good to see you home again, Anne.'

Anne felt a rush of gratitude towards her sister-in-law. At least Helen had welcomed her as though she really was pleased to see her again.

'Look,' said Helen, showing her a small diamond sparkling on her engagement finger. 'Didn't I tell you? I won my bet, but only after the most awful row. I must say, I enjoyed it though. Mummy and Francis were both livid.'

Anne drew a deep breath. Didn't Helen also know that her own holiday had been cut short because of that ring?

'So Roger Baxter has won after all,' she said heavily, and Helen's eyes sparkled again with mischief.

'Roger Baxter? Of course not, Anne darling. You didn't *really* think it was Roger, did you? I'm engaged to Peter . . . you know, Peter Birkett.'

Sheer bewilderment kept Anne silent. She had met the tall quiet man with the crisp dark hair who was their vet, and who often came to examine the horses, and she liked him very much.

But Helen . . . Helen had never given any hint of a love affair between them! She stared at the smiling mischievous face.

'If you want Mummy to agree to something, then offer her an alternative she won't like at all. It always works. Peter hated my methods and we rowed about it sometimes . . . but I was right. You should have heard them when they thought it was Roger! Francis likes Peter, though . . . and so does Mummy, come to that.'

'I've never heard anything so . . . so outrageous,' Anne told her, when she got her breath back. 'Why on earth bring Roger Baxter in when there was no need?'

'I've just told you, darling.'

Anne remembered that she was supposed to be the alternative to Caroline . . . on Helen's advice!

'No doubt you think it a pity it didn't work with Francis and me,' she said, her eyes stormy, and Helen's laughter faded.

'No, Anne,' she said quietly. 'Oddly enough, I don't think that any more. I'm glad Francis chose you.'

Francis' voice interrupted as he walked downstairs, and both girls turned to look up at him.

'I would like to talk to you, Anne, when you've refreshed yourself after the journey. That is . . . if you aren't too tired. If you'd rather, it will keep till tomorrow.'

'No, I'll come to the study after dinner,' Anne told him. 'I'll just say hello to your mother. I . . . '

She turned back to Helen. It was no good discussing the engagement further, when Francis so obviously wanted to talk to her about it. Perhaps he wasn't as happy about it as Helen believed.

Yet what could she say? She could have supported Francis if he wanted to make Helen think twice about Roger Baxter, whom she had never managed to like.

But Peter Birkett was a fine man, and Helen was lucky to be marrying him. She could see that the girl was in love, and probably they had both been in love all along. She could imagine Peter Birkett would hate Helen's methods, as she put it, but it seemed to have worked, judging by the girl's radiant face.

As she climbed upstairs to freshen up, Anne felt rather apprehensive. In this case, she and Francis were probably going to be on opposing sides.

Judith was with her mother in her

favourite room, her own frilly bedroom. She was chattering happily while Mrs. Wyatt was busy sorting through some clothes. Anne was surprised when the older woman suddenly came to meet her and kissed her cheek.

'Welcome home again, Anne dear,' she said. 'We've missed you. Francis told me about Judith . . . and now she's telling me herself. I . . . I don't mind telling you, it's a relief. I was so afraid that there was something wrong with the child, I couldn't even bring myself to admit the possibility deep down, even to myself. It's been worrying me. But Judith says your friend thinks it may just be wax in her ears.'

'Quite right,' said Anne. 'He's pretty sure it's only wax. We must see her doctor, though. Could you send for him as soon as possible?'

'I'll ring straight away and leave a message. I . . . I never thought of her hearing. I . . .'

There was a small break in her voice, and again Anne had to overcome her surprise. Mrs. Wyatt had always seemed so aloof and self-contained, but now it was as though a barrier had been broken down.

In many ways Francis was like her, thought Anne wonderingly. He, too, seemed to be behind a barrier.

'There's to be a jumble sale at the Church Hall,' Mrs. Wyatt was explaining. 'I'm sorting through my clothes. Have you anything you don't want, Anne?'

'Perhaps.'

She thought of a few clothes which she would soon be unable to wear, and which would no doubt be sadly out of fashion by another year.

'Put them on this bundle, then, dear. Mrs. Hansett is going to get Hansett to take them over to the Church Hall in the Land Rover. I should have done this during the week, but I forgot.'

Anne couldn't keep back a smile.

'All right,' she agreed, 'though I must wash before we have dinner.'

'It's nice having a busy table again in

the evening,' said her mother-in-law with a sigh. 'I didn't realise till you left that I liked it that way. I must be getting old, Anne, and I'm beginning to realise there's much to be said for a back seat.'

'Don't say that,' said Anne unthinkingly. 'You may need to take a front one again shortly.'

'Why is that?'

Anne turned away quickly, realising how easy it was to give away her secret. Soon, too, it could no longer be kept a secret, she thought, looking at her belt which needed a new latch.

'There's enough work here for both of us,' she said evasively. 'I'll get those dresses.'

10

Francis was sitting at his desk when Anne finally went to talk to him after the high tea which they often had instead of dinner. A log fire had been lit as the evening had grown chilly, and Anne looked out on the lovely long view across the park, now dulled behind scudding clouds, but strangely beautiful in all weathers. The picnic, that afternoon, seemed years away instead of a few hours.

'Your flowers are dying, Francis,' she said, pulling out withered roses from a large floral arrangement on the table. 'I'll have to do another one for you tomorrow.'

'Never mind the flowers, Anne,' he said as he rose from behind the desk. 'Sit down for a moment, please.'

She sat down and he came to sit opposite to her, kicking at a log on the fire. The flames drew deep lines down his face, and made his eyes glow sombrely.

'Why didn't you tell me about the child, Anne?' he asked, and she stared at him, bewildered.

'I didn't know she was losing her hearing,' she defended. 'Surely you know that. It was Graham who spotted it.'

'Don't prevaricate,' he said wearily. 'I mean our child, of course.'

She felt the blood drain from her face.

'How do you know?'

He shrugged. 'Does it matter?'

It did matter! Anne had a sudden vision of Graham talking quickly to Francis while she waited in the car at the picnic. She had thought he was explaining Judith's condition, but now she knew he had also been explaining hers!

'How could Graham tell you!' she cried. 'How could he betray my confidence?'

She saw the dark blood mounting his face.

'You told Lord, then, when you couldn't tell me!'

He got up and walked about the room.

'You had parted with Graham Lord *before* I asked you to marry me,' he reminded her. 'I didn't come between you. Yet you run to him now. You and he . . . did you find out you'd made a mistake in parting from one another? Was that it, Anne? Are you still bound to your old love?'

She felt anger stirring as a vision of Caroline Cook rose before her, the girl looking young and defenceless, and bewildered by Francis's sudden change towards her.

'How dare you ask me that!' she cried, 'when you yourself are still bound to *your* old love. What about Caroline Cook? You loved her, didn't you, then all of a sudden you married me. You didn't explain to her, did you, Francis? You left her utterly bewildered. Why did you marry me when you were still bound, morally at least, to another girl?'

He was staring at her, white-faced.

'You believe that of me? You . . . '

'Caroline isn't the sort of girl to be treated lightly, Francis,' Anne went on without heeding. 'Maybe . . . maybe you all felt she wasn't quite right for mistress of Elvan, but . . . but by birth I'm no better, nor has Helen chosen any better, come to that. But surely no one is old-fashioned enough to set a great deal of store by suitable marriages these days! Surely one should marry for love, nothing else.'

She broke off abruptly, feeling she could have bitten out her tongue. Had she given herself away completely?

'You didn't marry for love, did you?' Francis asked, his eyes brightly hard.

'Nor did you,' she flashed, and he was silent.

'I can't let you go,' he told her, 'even if you have made a mistake, and want Graham Lord now, I can't let you go. Our child must come first now, Anne.'

'Was that what you wanted?' she asked bitterly. 'An heir for Elvan? You married a mistress for Elvan, and now you can have an heir. That ought to satisfy you.'

'It ought to,' Francis repeated.

But she could see that it didn't. He thought she had made a mistake over Graham, but it was his own thoughts which were pointing him in that direction. Was he now regretting Caroline? She looked at him and saw the lost, rather helpless look back on his face again, as he bent to throw another log on the fire.

'Let's think about Judith, not about us,' she said, more gently.

'Aren't you happy ... about our baby?' he asked, and she could feel his eyes searching her face. If only things had been different, how happy she would have been!

'Of course,' she said quickly, and refused to meet his eyes.

For a moment his hand gripped her shoulder till it pained her, then she felt his hold loosen.

'It's getting late, Anne. It's been a very long day and you must be tired. I'll see that you have as much help as you need in the house. Mrs. Hansett will arrange it.'

'Don't go treating me like an invalid,' she said crossly. 'I shall carry on normally for several months yet.'

The words lay between them, then Francis turned away awkwardly.

'You know best . . . about these things.'

She felt tears grip her throat as she walked out of the study. The news of their baby should not have been discussed like that, with anger and distrust between them. If they hadn't love, at least they'd had liking and respect. Yet now it seemed that everything had gone, and only a shred of toleration remained.

Yet they must make it work, for their baby's sake. But how? wondered Anne. How could they ever be happy in their marriage?

It was Anne and Francis who took Judith to a special clinic, arranged by her doctor, to have her ears examined and syringed. As Graham had suspected, the loss of hearing had been caused by hardened wax, and very soon Judith could hear again perfectly, if too loudly for comfort.

'That will pass quickly,' they were told, 'then she'll be perfectly all right.'

Anne rejoiced to see the little girl so well and happy again, and Francis asked Judith what she would like to do before they went home.

'Go down to Keswick to my favourite coffee shop, and have coffee and cakes,' she said happily.

'Very well, young lady,' Francis agreed, and drove south through Embleton to Bassenthwaite Lake, and along the narrow road which skirted the Lake to Keswick. It was a run which never failed to please Anne, and she felt strangely contented as they parked the car, and made their way towards the quaint old coffee house. Francis, too, looked cheerful, though now and again his eyes rested on Anne broodingly.

'Can I also get some Kendal Mint Cake,' Judith was asking, 'and take rum butter home to Mummy? She loves it.'

'There's a word for young ladies who trade in on things,' said Francis severely, though his eyes were suddenly twinkling when they met Anne's. If only he was always like this, she thought, rather sadly.

They had told the rest of the household about the coming baby, and Anne had also written to her parents. They had been showered with congratulations which had been bitter-sweet to Anne, as she carried a small knot of unhappiness inside her which, she felt, would always be with her. It made her very conscious of the barrier which stood between her and Francis.

Now they both watched silently, while Judith chose boxes of sweets and tubs of rum butter to take home.

'I . . . I'd like to thank you for helping

Judith,' Francis said awkwardly, leaning towards her.

'I did nothing,' she told him.

'Only took the proper interest in her. You've made a difference to my home, Anne. It . . . it feels like home now. I was going to ask you . . . '

He broke off as Judith came back to their table, and Anne felt her heart beating rather fast. There had been something different in Francis' voice when he spoke to her. There had been a more personal note.

'I've got fudge for me and for you, too, Anne, and brandy butter for Francis.'

'Thank you very much,' smiled Anne, though she wasn't very fond of fudge.

'Oh, look!' cried Judith suddenly. 'There's Caroline . . . and David Mellor.'

Anne looked hastily out of the window, catching a glimpse of the small dainty girl, her dark hair streaming on her shoulders, and the young groom holding her arm. She remembered long ago over-hearing part of a conversation between them. Could Caroline be getting over her love for Francis? she wondered, and glanced at his face.

Once again the shutters were down and he looked grim. Anne's heart sank. Whatever Francis felt for Caroline, it was still with him, even if Caroline was beginning to forget.

'Come on,' she said, suddenly reaching for her handbag. 'Can't we go home now?'

'Of course,' said Francis, rising. 'I'll just pay the bill.'

Anne found the small pair of embroidery scissors next day, as she examined an old chair in the morning, wondering if she ought to buy loose covers.

For a long moment she looked at them, then she decided to walk over to Cravenhill and return them. It was odd that Caroline had not rung up to ask for them, though she may not have missed them yet.

Francis was again in Carlisle and the

household had settled down to a steady routine. Mrs. Hansett was obviously happy, fussing a little over Anne, and Helen was excitedly planning her wedding with her mother, who was beginning to spend less and less time in her own room. She wanted plenty of frills for the wedding, and Helen was willing to indulge her.

'Mummy loves having all the trimmings,' she confided to Anne. 'It was Daddy who hated fuss, and Francis is just like him. But he'll have to put up with it for my wedding. We aren't all like him . . . sorry, Anne.'

'That's all right,' said Anne equably. She was no longer annoyed by Helen's tactless remarks.

But now she put on her anorak after lunch and wrapped up the scissors in a polythene bag. She would walk over to Cravenhill. The exercise would do her good.

Once again she found that Caroline was helping with the farm work, and

Beatrice Cook asked her to sit down and wait.

'Caroline is down in the long field, seeing to the hens, Mrs. Wyatt.'

'Then would you mind if I just walk down there?' asked Anne. 'I can't spend too much time on my errand.'

'Not at all,' said Beatrice.

★ ★ ★

Caroline flushed deeply when she saw Anne walking towards her, and rubbed her hands awkwardly down her jeans, looking deeply embarrassed.

'I've brought your scissors back,' Anne explained, feeling sorry to have taken the girl by surprise. 'I expect you'll need them soon.'

'Monday,' Caroline told her, her head going down, 'I travel to London on Sunday.'

There was a long awkward pause, while Anne began to feel as acutely uncomfortable as the other girl.

'I expect you really came to ask me

why I did it,' Caroline said at length. 'I . . . I can only say I'm sorry. I guess I was a little bit mad . . . I can see that now. David has made me see things so much more clearly, and it was wicked of me to try to harm you, especially when I broke your confidence that way.'

Anne felt her legs wobble a little and sat down suddenly on the grass, while Caroline stood looking down at her. Caroline had broken her confidence. Did that mean . . . ?

'Francis was furious when I told him . . . about the baby, I mean. I thought he would be, if I told him instead of you, and I wanted to make him angry with you. It was the only thing I could think of left to do. Only I could see he was delighted, too.'

'*You* told him!' cried Anne.

Caroline nodded.

'I was going to tell you before I left.' Tears were beginning to thicken her voice. 'I'm not proud of myself. I was the one who kept chasing Francis, you see. I pretended to myself he wanted me, too, and often I felt that this was really true. Only, now that I'm honest with myself, I can see it was all on my side. Francis never wanted me. To him I was just Helen's best friend. He must have wanted you instead and I . . . I was jealous and when I knew you hadn't told him . . . about the baby, I mean . . . I told him instead because I thought it would make trouble between you.'

And it had, thought Anne, feeling cold inside. She looked up at the girl who had told her so many lies. Why had she believed her instead of Francis? And why hadn't Francis told her it was Caroline who broke her confidence? Instead he had been furious when he thought she had confided in Graham, too!

Anne rose to her feet. She had heard enough.

'Francis didn't tell me it was you,' she said heavily.

'Oh no, he wouldn't! He's awfully old-fashioned in some ways, especially about women. He'd never put the blame on a woman for anything.'

Except on me, thought Anne, remembering the panelling and other small incidents.

'I guess you despise me,' said Caroline. 'I . . . I hope the baby is a boy.'

'Thank you,' said Anne, and turned away. Now she only wanted to get home.

★ ★ ★

Francis was late that evening and it wasn't until they were upstairs that Anne had a chance to talk to him. She heard him come up to bed, and tapped lightly on the dividing door before going into the room.

'Can I talk to you, Francis?'

He looked at her for a moment as she stood tall and straight, her fair hair hanging long and shining to her shoulders, a new soft bloom on her checks.

'What is it?' he asked, rather wearily, and she hesitated.

'I . . . I owe you an apology,' she began rather stiffly.

'I don't want any more apologies.'

'Nevertheless I must give it,' she insisted. 'I blamed you . . . for Caroline Cook, but I know now that it was all just in her imagination. She's been good enough . . . if you can call it that . . . to tell me so.'

'Would that have made any difference?' asked Francis. 'Would it suddenly have made you love me when you're already in love with someone else?'

'Someone? Graham, you mean?'

'Of course.'

'I don't love Graham.'

She came towards him, knowing that there could only be honesty between them now.

'I love you, Francis. If you really must know, I broke it off with Graham because of you. I loved you long before you asked me to marry you. That's why

. . . why I accepted you. I . . . realise that though you don't care for Caroline and haven't ever encouraged her, it . . . it doesn't mean that you care for me, though. I . . . I thought I had enough love for both of us . . . only it didn't seem to work that way.'

He was staring at her incredulously, then with dawning belief in his eyes as he came to draw her into his arms.

'Anne darling, there's a lot you're saying that doesn't make sense, but I hope I heard right when you say you love me. What a lot of time we've wasted! Why couldn't you have said so before? I . . . '

'You didn't ask me, and besides, I thought you really did love Caroline. She's so pretty.'

'But not beautiful, like you. And anyway, why should I marry you, if I loved Caroline?'

'You never said you loved me, though, Francis. I . . . I thought you didn't.'

'I was so afraid of scaring you off. I

married you quickly after Graham Lord, in case someone else snapped you up. I . . . I'm not good at paying court to the ladies, Anne. I only ever fell in love with you, you see.'

Suddenly Anne was laughing help-lessly, and Francis, after a moment, joined in.

'I was so jealous of Lord, too,' he told her drawing her close. 'I could have killed him when I saw him holding your hand, and when I thought you'd told him about our baby . . . before me!'

'He's a doctor. He didn't have to be told,' said Anne. 'I tried to tell you, Francis, really I did. Only it seemed like buying your love, and I thought you only wanted a mistress for Elvan.'

'I prefer a wife,' said Francis, and this time Anne believed him.

Mary Jane Warmington
is a pseudonym of Mary Cummins
who also writes as Jane Carrick.

We do hope that you have enjoyed reading this large print book.

Did you know that all of our titles are available for purchase?

We publish a wide range of high quality large print books including:
Romances, Mysteries, Classics, General Fiction, Non Fiction and Westerns.

Special interest titles available in large print are:
The Little Oxford Dictionary Music Book, Song Book Hymn Book, Service Book

Also available from us courtesy of Oxford University Press:
Young Readers' Dictionary (large print edition) Young Readers' Thesaurus (large print edition)

For further information or a free brochure, please contact us at:
**Ulverscroft Large Print Books Ltd., The Green, Bradgate Road, Anstey, Leicester, LE7 7FU, England.
Tel:** (00 44) **0116 236 4325
Fax:** (00 44) **0116 234 0205**